O HENRY - No Story & Other Short Stories

William Sidney Porter was born in Greensboro, North Carolina on September 11, 1862 He was a voracious reader as a child reading anything and everything from classics to cheap dime store novels.

He graduated from his aunt's elementary school in 1876 and then enrolled at the Lindsey Street High School though his aunt continued to tutor him until he was fifteen.

At age 17 in 1879 he started working in his uncle's drugstore and two years later he was licensed as a pharmacist. As a sideshow he would sketch the passing townsfolk.

Porter travelled to Texas in March 1882, hoping a change of air would help relieve a persistent cough.

In Austin he led an active social life as well as singing and playing both guitar and mandolin. He became a member of the "Hill City Quartet," and through this began courting Athol Estes, then seventeen and from a wealthy family. Her mother objected to the match because Athol was suffering from tuberculosis. On July 1, 1887, Porter eloped with Athol.

The couple continued with musical and theater groups, with Athol encouraging Porter to pursue his writing. 1n 1888 Athol gave birth to a son who died hours after birth. 1n 1889, a daughter, Margaret Worth Porter, was born.

Porter's friend Richard Hall became Texas Land Commissioner and offered Porter a job as a draftsman at the Texas General Land Office (GLO) in 1887 at a salary of $100 a month, drawing maps from surveys and field notes. As a developing and popular writer he continued to contribute to magazines and newspapers.

Porter resigned from the GLO in early 1891 and began working at the First National Bank of Austin as a teller and bookkeeper. The bank was informally run and Porter was careless in keeping his books and was fired for suspected embezzlement.

He next went to work full time on his humorous weekly called The Rolling Stone, which he started while working at the bank. The Rolling Stone featured satire on life, people and politics and included Porter's short stories and sketches. Although eventually reaching a top circulation of 1500, The Rolling Stone failed in April 1895. However, his writing and drawings had caught the attention of the editor at the Houston Post.

Porter and his family moved to Houston in 1895, where he started writing for the Post. His salary was only $25 a month, but rose steadily. Porter gathered ideas for his column by loitering in hotel lobbies and observing and talking to people there.

While he was in Houston, the First National Bank of Austin was audited by federal auditors and they found the embezzlement that had led to his firing. A federal indictment followed and he was arrested on charges of embezzlement. Porter's father-in-law posted bail to keep Porter out of jail. Porter was due to stand trial on July 7, 1896, but the day before he fled, first to New Orleans and then Honduras. Whilst in Trujillo for several months he wrote Cabbages and Kings, in which he coined the term "banana republic" to describe the country.

Porter had sent Athol and Margaret back to Austin to live with Athol's parents. Unfortunately, Athol became too ill to meet Porter in Honduras as Porter had planned. When he learned that his wife was dying, Porter returned to Austin in February 1897 and surrendered to the court, pending an appeal. Once again, Porter's father-in-law posted bail so Porter could stay with Athol and Margaret.

Athol Estes Porter died on July 25, 1897, from tuberculosis. Porter was found guilty of embezzlement in February 1898 and sentenced to five years in prison as federal prisoner 30664 in Columbus, Ohio. There, Porter, as a licensed pharmacist, worked in the prison hospital as the night druggist and given his own room in the hospital wing. There he had fourteen stories published under various pseudonyms, but was becoming best known as "O. Henry", a pseudonym that first appeared with the story "Whistling Dick's Christmas Stocking" in the December 1899 issue of McClure's Magazine. Porter was released in July 1901, for good behavior after serving three years.

Porter reunited with his daughter Margaret, now age 11, in Pittsburgh, Pennsylvania, where Athol's parents had moved after Porter's conviction.

Porter's most prolific writing period began in 1902, in New York City. While there, he wrote 381 short stories. His wit, characterization, and plot twists were loved by his readers but panned by critics.

In 1907 Porter married childhood sweetheart Sarah (Sallie) Lindsey Coleman, whom he met again after revisiting his native state of North Carolina.

Porter was a heavy drinker, and his health deteriorated markedly in 1908, which affected his writing. In 1909, Sarah left him, and he died on June 5, 1910, of cirrhosis of the liver, complications of diabetes, and an enlarged heart. After funeral services in New York City, he was buried in the Riverside Cemetery in Asheville, North Carolina.

Index Of Stories

"THE ROSE OF DIXIE"
When The Rose of Dixie magazine was started by a stock company in Toombs City, Georgia, there was never but one candidate for its chief editorial position in the minds of its owners. Col. Aquila Telfair was the man for the place. By all the rights of learning, family, reputation, and Southern traditions, he was its foreordained, fit, and logical editor. So, a committee of the patriotic Georgia citizens who had subscribed the founding fund of $100,000 called upon Colonel Telfair at his residence, Cedar Heights, fearful lest the enterprise and the South should suffer by his possible refusal.

The colonel received them in his great library, where he spent most of his days. The library had descended to him from his father. It contained ten thousand volumes, some of which had been published as late as the year 1861. When the deputation arrived, Colonel Telfair was seated at his massive white-pine centre-table, reading Burton's Anatomy of Melancholy. He arose and shook hands punctiliously with each member of the committee. If you were familiar with The Rose of Dixie you will remember the colonel's portrait, which appeared in it from time to time. You could not forget the long, carefully brushed white hair; the hooked, high-bridged nose, slightly twisted to the left; the keen eyes under the still black eyebrows; the classic mouth beneath the drooping white mustache, slightly frazzled at the ends.

The committee solicitously offered him the position of managing editor, humbly presenting an outline of the field that the publication was designed to cover and mentioning a comfortable salary. The colonel's lands were growing poorer each year and were much cut up by red gullies. Besides, the honor was not one to be refused.

In a forty-minute speech of acceptance, Colonel Telfair gave an outline of English literature from Chaucer to Macaulay, re-fought the battle of Chancellorsville, and said that, God helping him, he would so conduct The Rose of Dixie that its fragrance and beauty would permeate the entire world, hurling back into the teeth of the Northern minions their belief that no genius or good could exist in the brains and hearts of the people whose property they had destroyed and whose rights they had curtailed.

Offices for the magazine were partitioned off and furnished in the second floor of the First National Bank building; and it was for the colonel to cause The Rose of Dixie to blossom and flourish or to wilt in the balmy air of the land of flowers.

The staff of assistants and contributors that Editor-Colonel Telfair drew about him was a peach. It was a whole crate of Georgia peaches. The first assistant editor, Tolliver Lee Fairfax, had had a father killed during Pickett's charge. The second assistant, Keats Unthank, was the nephew of one of Morgan's Raiders. The book reviewer, Jackson Rockingham, had been the youngest soldier in the Confederate army, having appeared on the field of battle with a sword in one hand and a milk-bottle in the other. The art editor, Roncesvalles Sykes, was a third cousin to a nephew of Jefferson Davis. Miss Lavinia Terhune, the colonel's stenographer and typewriter, had an aunt who had once been kissed by Stonewall Jackson. Tommy Webster, the head office-boy, got his job by having recited Father Ryan's poems, complete, at the commencement exercises of the Toombs City High School. The girls who wrapped and addressed the magazines were members of old Southern families in Reduced Circumstances. The cashier was a scrub named Hawkins, from Ann Arbor, Michigan, who had recommendations and a bond
from a guarantee company filed with the owners. Even Georgia stock companies sometimes realize that it takes live ones to bury the dead.

Well, sir, if you believe me, The Rose of Dixie blossomed five times before anybody heard of it except the people who buy their hooks and eyes in Toombs City. Then Hawkins climbed off his stool and told on 'em to the stock company. Even in Ann Arbor he had been used to having his business propositions heard of at least as far away as Detroit. So an advertising manager was engaged - Beauregard Fitzhugh Banks, a young man in a lavender necktie, whose grandfather had been the Exalted High Pillow-slip of the Kuklux Klan.

In spite of which The Rose of Dixie kept coming out every month. Although in every issue it ran photos of either the Taj Mahal or the Luxembourg Gardens, or Carmencita or La Follette, a certain number of people bought it and subscribed for it. As a boom for it, Editor-Colonel Telfair ran three different views of Andrew Jackson's old home, "The Hermitage," a full-page engraving of the second battle of Manassas, entitled "Lee to the Rear!" and a five-thousand-word biography of Belle Boyd in the same number. The subscription list that month advanced 118. Also there were poems in the same issue by Leonina Vashti Haricot (pen-name), related to the Haricots of Charleston, South Carolina, and Bill Thompson, nephew of one of the stockholders. And an article from a special society correspondent describing a tea-party given by the swell Boston and English set, where a lot of tea was spilled overboard by some of the guests masquerading as Indians.

One day a person whose breath would easily cloud a mirror, he was so much alive, entered the office of The Rose of Dixie. He was a man about the size of a real-estate agent, with a self-tied tie and a manner that he must have borrowed conjointly from W J. Bryan, Hackenschmidt, and Hetty Green. He was shown into the editor-colonel's pons asinorum. Colonel Telfair rose and began a Prince Albert bow.

"I'm Thacker," said the intruder, taking the editor's chair "T. T. Thacker, of New York."

He dribbled hastily upon the colonel's desk some cards, a bulky manila envelope, and a letter from the owners of The Rose of Dixie. This letter introduced Mr. Thacker, and politely requested Colonel Telfair to give him a conference and whatever information about the magazine he might desire.

"I've been corresponding with the secretary of the magazine owners for some time," said Thacker, briskly. "I'm a practical magazine man myself, and a circulation booster as good as any, if I do say it. I'll guarantee an increase of anywhere from ten thousand to a hundred thousand a year for any publication that isn't printed in a dead language. I've had my eye on The Rose of Dixie ever since it started. I know every end of the business from editing to setting up the classified ads. Now, I've come down here to put a good bunch of money in the magazine, if I can see my way clear. It ought to be made to pay. The secretary tells me it's losing money. I don't see why a magazine in the South, if it's properly handled, shouldn't get a good circulation in the North, too.

"Colonel Telfair leaned back in his chair and polished his gold-rimmed glasses.

"Mr. Thacker," said he, courteously but firmly, "The Rose of Dixie is a publication devoted to the fostering and the voicing of Southern genius. Its watchword, which you may have seen on the cover, is 'Of, For, and By the South.'"

"But you wouldn't object to a Northern circulation, would you?" asked Thacker.

"I suppose," said the editor-colonel, "that it is customary to open the circulation lists to all. I do not know. I have nothing to do with the business affairs of the magazine. I was called upon to assume editorial control of it, and I have devoted to its conduct such poor literary talents as I may possess and whatever store of erudition I may have acquired."

"Sure," said Thacker. "But a dollar is a dollar anywhere, North, South, or West - whether you're buying codfish, goober peas, or Rocky Ford cantaloupes. Now, I've been looking over your November number. I see one here on your desk. You don't mind running over it with me?

"Well, your leading article is all right. A good write-up of the cotton-belt with plenty of photographs is a winner any time. New York is always interested in the cotton crop. And this sensational account of Hatfield-McCoy feud, by a schoolmate of a niece of the Governor of Kentucky, isn't such a bad idea. It happened so long ago that most people have forgotten it. Now, here's a poem three pages long called 'The Tyrant's Foot,' by Lorella Lascelles. I've pawed around a good deal over manuscripts, but I never saw her name on a rejection slip."

"Miss Lascelles," said the editor, "is one of our most widely recognized Southern poetesses. She is closely related to the Alabama Lascelles family, and made with her own hands the silken Confederate banner that was presented to the governor of that state at his inauguration."

"But why," persisted Thacker, "is the poem illustrated with a view of the M. & 0. Railroad freight depot at Tuscaloosa?"

"The illustration," said the colonel, with dignity, "shows a corner of the fence surrounding the old homestead where Miss Lascelles was born."

"All right," said Thacker. "I read the poem, but I couldn't tell whether it was about the depot of the battle of Bull Run. Now, here's a short story called 'Rosies' Temptation,' by Fosdyke Piggott. It's rotten. What is a Piggott, anyway?"

"Mr. Piggott," said the editor, "is a brother of the principal stockholder of the magazine."

"All's right with the world, Piggott passes," said Thacker. "Well this article on Arctic exploration and the one on tarpon fishing might go. But how about this write-up of the Atlanta, New Orleans, Nashville, and Savannah breweries? It seems to consist mainly of statistics about their output and the quality of their beer. What's the chip over the bug?"

"If I understand your figurative language," answered Colonel Telfair, "it is this: the article you refer to was handed to me by the owners of the magazine with instructions to publish it. The literary quality of it did not appeal to me. But, in a measure, I feel impelled to conform, in certain matters, to the wishes of the gentlemen who are interested in the financial side of The Rose."

"I see," said Thacker. "Next we have two pages of selections from 'Lalla Rookh,' by Thomas Moore. Now, what Federal prison did Moore escape from, or what's the name of the F. F. V. family that he carries as a handicap?"

"Moore was an Irish poet who died in 1852," said Colonel Telfair, pityingly. "He is a classic. I have been thinking of reprinting his translation of Anacreon serially in the magazine."

"Look out for the copyright laws," said Thacker, flippantly. Who's Bessie Belleclair, who contributes the essay on the newly completed water-works plant in Milledgeville?"

"The name, sir," said Colonel Telfair, "is the nom de guerre of Miss Elvira Simpkins. I have not the honor of knowing the lady; but her contribution was sent to us by Congressman Brower, of her native state. Congressman Brower's mother was related to the Polks of Tennessee.

"Now, see here, Colonel," said Thacker, throwing down the magazine, "this won't do. You can't successfully run a magazine for one particular section of the country. You've got to make a universal appeal. Look how the Northern publications have catered to the South and encouraged the Southern writers. And you've got to go far and wide for your contributors. You've got to buy stuff according to its quality without any regard to the pedigree of the author. Now, I'll bet a quart of ink that this Southern parlor organ you've been running has never played a note that originated about Mason & Hamlin's line. Am I right?"

"I have carefully and conscientiously rejected all contributions from that section of the country, if I understand your figurative language aright," replied the colonel.

"All right. Now I'll show you something."

Thacker reached for his thick manila envelope and dumped a mass of typewritten manuscript on the editors desk.

"Here's some truck," said he, "that I paid cash for, and brought along with me."

One by one he folded back the manuscripts and showed their first pages to the colonel.

Here are four short stories four of the highest priced authors in the United States - three of 'em living in New York, and one commuting. There's a special article on Vienna-bred society by Tom Vampson. Here's an Italian serial by Captain Jack – no - it's the other Crawford. Here are three separate exposes of city governments by Sniffings, and here's a dandy entitled 'What Women Carry in Dress-Suit Cases' a Chicago newspaper woman hired herself out for five years as a lady's maid to get that information. And here's a Synopsis of Preceding Chapters of Hall Caine's new serial to appear next June. And here's a couple of pounds of vers de societe that I got at a rate from the clever magazines. That's the stuff that people everywhere want. And now here's a writeup with photographs at the ages of four, twelve, twenty-two, and thirty of George B. McClellan. It's a prognostication. He's bound to be elected Mayor of New York. It '11 make a big hit all over the country. He -"

"I beg your pardon," said Colonel Telfair, stiffening in his chair. "What was the name?"

"Oh, I see," said Thacker, with half a grin. Yes, he's a son of the General. We'll pass that manuscript up. But, if you'll excuse me, Colonel, it's a magazine we're trying to make go off, not the first gun at Fort Sumter. Now, here's a thing that's bound to get next to you. It's an original poem by James Whitcomb Riley. J.W. himself. You know what that means to a magazine. I won't tell you what I had to pay for that poem; but I'll tell you this, Riley can make more money writing with a fountain-pen than you or I can with one that lets the ink run. I'll read you the last two stanzas:

"'Pa lays around 'n' loafs all day,
'N' reads and makes us leave him be.
He lets me do just like I please,
'N' when I'm in bad he laughs at me,
'N' when I holler loud 'n' say
Bad words 'n' then begin to tease
The cat, 'n' pa just smiles, ma's mad
'N' gives me Jesse crost her knees.
I always wondered why that wuz-
I guess it's cause
Pa never does.

""'N' after all the lights are out
I'm sorry 'bout it; so I creep
Out of my trundle bed to ma's
'N' say I love her a whole heap,
'N' kiss her, 'n' I hug her tight.
'N' it's too dark to see her eyes,
But every time I do I know
She cries 'n' cries 'n' cries 'n' cries.
I always wondered why that wuz-
I guess it's 'cause
Pa never does.'

"That's the stuff," continued Thacker. "What do you think of that?"

"I am not unfamiliar with the works of Mr. Riley," said the colonel, deliberately. "I believe he lives in Indiana. For the last ten years I have been somewhat of a literary recluse, and am familiar with nearly all the books in the Cedar Heights library. I am also of the opinion that a magazine should contain a certain amount of poetry. Many of the sweetest singers of the South have already contributed to the pages of The Rose of Dixie. I, myself, have thought of translating from the original for publication in its pages the works of the great Italian poet Tasso. Have you ever drunk from the fountain of this immortal poet's lines, Mr. Thacker?"

"Not even a demi-Tasso," said Thacker.

Now, let's come to the point, Colonel Telfair. I've already invested some money in this as a flyer. That bunch of manuscripts cost me $4,000. My object was to try a number of them in the next issue-I believe you make up less than a month ahead and see what effect it has on the circulation. I believe that by printing the best stuff we can get in the North, South, East, or West we can make the magazine go. You have there the letter from the owning company asking you to co-operate with me in the plan. Let's chuck out some of this slush that you've been publishing just because the writers are related to the Skoopdoodles of Skoopdoodle County. Are you with me?"

"As long as I continue to be the editor of The Rose," said Colonel Telfair, with dignity, "I shall be its editor. But I desire also to conform to the wishes of its owners if I can do so conscientiously."

"That's the talk," said Thacker, briskly. "Now, how much of this stuff I've brought can we get into the January number? We want to begin right away."

"There is yet space in the January number," said the editor, "for about eight thousand words, roughly estimated."

"Great!" said Thacker. "It isn't much, but it'll give the readers some change from goobers, governors, and Gettysburg. I'll leave the selection of the stuff I brought to fill the space to you, as it's all good. I've got to run back to New York, and I'll be down again in a couple of weeks."

Colonel Telfair slowly swung his eye-glasses by their broad, black ribbon.

"The space in the January number that I referred to," said he, measuredly, "has been held open purposely, pending a decision that I have not yet made. A short time ago a contribution was submitted to The Rose of Dixie that is one of the most remarkable literary efforts that has ever come under my observation. None but a master mind and talent could have produced it. It would just fill the space that I have reserved for its possible use."

Thacker looked anxious.

"What kind of stuff is it?" he asked. "Eight thousand words sounds suspicious. The oldest families must have been collaborating. Is there going to be another secession ?"

"The author of the article," continued the colonel, ignoring Thacker's allusions, "is a writer of some reputation. He has also distinguished himself in other ways. I do not feel at liberty to reveal to you his name - at least not until I have decided whether or not to accept his contribution."

"Well," said Thacker, nervously, "is it a continued story, or an account of the unveiling of the new town pump in Whitmire, South Carolina, or a revised list of General Lee's body-servants, or what?"

"You are disposed to be facetious," said Colonel Telfair, calmly. "The article is from the pen of a thinker, a philosopher, a lover of mankind, a student, and a rhetorician of high degree."

"It must have been written by a syndicate," said Thacker. "But, honestly, Colonel, you want to go slow. I don't know of any eight-thousand-word single doses of written matter that are read by anybody these days, except Supreme Court briefs and reports of murder trials. You haven't by any accident gotten hold of a copy of one of Daniel Webster's speeches, have you?"

Colonel Telfair swung a little in his chair and looked steadily from under his bushy eyebrows at the magazine promoter.

"Mr. Thacker," he said, gravely, "I am willing to segregate the somewhat crude expression of your sense of humor from the solicitude that your business investments undoubtedly have conferred upon you. But I must ask you to cease your jibes and derogatory comments upon the South and the Southern people. They, sir, will not be tolerated in the office of The Rose of Dixie for one moment. And before you proceed with more of your covert insinuations that I, the editor of this magazine, am not a competent judge of the merits of the matter submitted to its consideration, I beg that you will first present some evidence or proof that you are my superior in any way, shape, or form relative to the question in hand."

"Oh, come, Colonel," said Thacker, good-naturedly. "I didn't do anything like that to you. It sounds like an indictment by the fourth assistant attorney-general. Let's get back to business. What's this 8,000 to 1 shot about?"

"The article," said Colonel Telfair, acknowledging the apology by a slight bow, "covers a wide area of knowledge. It takes up theories and questions that have puzzled the world for centuries, and disposes of them logically and concisely. One by one it holds up to view the evils of the world, points out the way of eradicating them; and then conscientiously and in detail comments the good. There is hardly a phase of human life that it does not discuss wisely, calmly, and equitably. The great policies of governments, the duties of private citizens, the obligations of home life, law, ethics, morality, all these important subjects are handled with a calm wisdom and confidence that I must confess has captured my admiration."

"It must be a crackerjack," said Thacker, impressed.

"It is a great contribution to the world's wisdom," said the colonel.

"The only doubt remaining in my mind as to the tremendous advantage it would be to us to give it publication in The Rose of Dixie is that I have not yet sufficient information about the author to give his work publicity in our magazine.

"I thought you said he is a distinguished man," said Thacker.

"He is," replied the colonel, "both in literary and in other more diversified and extraneous fields. But I am extremely careful about the matter that I accept for publication. My contributors are people of unquestionable repute and connections, which fact can be verified at any time. As I said, I am holding this article until I can acquire more information about its author. I do not know whether I will publish it or not. If I decide against it, I shall be much pleased, Mr. Thacker, to substitute the matter that you are leaving with me in its place."

Thacker was somewhat at sea.

"I don't seem to gather," said he, "much about the gist of this inspired piece of literature. It sounds more like a dark horse than Pegasus to me."

"It is a human document," said the colonel-editor, confidently, "from a man of great accomplishments who, in my opinion, has obtained a stronger grasp on the world and its outcomes than that of any man living to-day."

Thacker rose to his feet excitedly.

"Say!" he said. "It isn't possible that you've cornered John D. Rockefeller's memoirs, is it? Don't tell me that all at once."

No, sir," said Colonel Telfair. "I am speaking of mentality and literature not of the less worthy intricacies of trade."

Well, what's the trouble about running the article," asked Thacker, a little impatiently, "if the man's well known and has got the stuff ?" Colonel Telfair sighed.

"Mr. Thacker," said he, "for once I have been tempted. Nothing has yet appeared in The Rose of Dixie that has not been from the pen of one of its sons or daughters. I know little about the author of this article except that he has acquired prominence in a section of the country that has always been inimical to my heart and mind. But I recognize his genius; and, as I have told you, I have instituted an investigation of his personality. Perhaps it will be futile. But I

shall pursue the inquiry. Until that is finished, I must leave open
the question of filling the vacant space in our January number."

Thacker arose to leave.

"All right, Colonel," he said, as cordially as he could. "You use your own
judgment. If you've really got a scoop or something that will make 'em
sit up, run it instead of my stuff. I'll drop in again in about two weeks.
Good luck!"

Colonel Telfair and the magazine promoter shook hands.

Returning a fortnight later, Thacker dropped off a very rocky Pullman
at Toombs City. He found the January number of the magazine made up
and the forms closed.

The vacant space that had been yawning for type was filled by an
article that was headed thus:

SECOND MESSAGE TO CONGRESS

Written for

THE ROSE OF DIXIE

BY

A Member of the Well-known

BULLOCH FAMILY, OF GEORGIA

T. Roosevelt

THE THIRD INGREDIENT

The (so-called) Vallambrosa Apartment-House is not an apartment-house.
It is composed of two old-fashioned, brownstone-front residences
welded into one. The parlor floor of one side is gay with the wraps
and head-gear of a modiste; the other is lugubrious with the sophistical
promises and grisly display of a painless dentist. You may have a room
there for two dollars a week or you may have one for twenty dollars.
Among the Vallambrosa's roomers are stenographers, musicians, brokers,
shop-girls, space-rate writers, art students, wire-tappers, and other
people who lean far over the banister-rail when the door-bell rings.

This treatise shall have to do with but two of the Vallambrosians, though meaning no disrespect to the others.

At six o'clock one afternoon Hetty Pepper came back to her third-floor rear $3.50 room in the Vallambrosa with her nose and chin more sharply pointed than usual. To be discharged from the department store where you have been working four years, and with only fifteen cents in your purse, does have a tendency to make your features appear more finely chiseled.

And now for Hetty's thumb-nail biography while she climbs the two flights of stairs.

She walked into the Biggest Store one morning four years before with seventy-five other girls, applying for a job behind the waist department counter. The phalanx of wage-earners formed a bewildering scene of beauty, carrying a total mass of blond hair sufficient to have justified the horseback gallops of a hundred Lady Godivas.

The capable, cool-eyed, impersonal, young, bald-headed man whose task it was to engage six of the contestants, was aware of a feeling of suffocation as if he were drowning in a sea of frangipanni, while white clouds, hand-embroidered, floated about him. And then a sail hove in sight. Hetty Pepper, homely of countenance, with small, contemptuous, green eyes and chocolate-colored hair, dressed in a suit of plain burlap and a common-sense hat, stood before him with every one of her twenty-nine years of life unmistakably in sight.

"You're on!." shouted the bald-headed young man, and was saved. And that is how Hetty came to be employed in the Biggest Store. The story of her rise to an eight-dollar-a-week salary is the combined stories of Hercules, Joan of Arc, Una, Job, and Little-Red-Riding-Hood. You shall not learn from me the salary that was paid her as a beginner. There is a sentiment growing about such things, and I want no millionaire store-proprietors climbing the fire-escape of my tenement-house to throw dynamite bombs into my skylight boudoir.

The story of Hetty's discharge from the Biggest Store is so nearly a repetition of her engagement as to be monotonous.

In each department of the store there is an omniscient, omnipresent, and omnivorous person carrying always a mileage book and a red necktie, and referred to as a "buyer." The destinies of the girls in his department who live on (see Bureau of Victual Statistics) so much per week are in his hands.

This particular buyer was a capable, cool-eyed, impersonal, young, bald-headed man. As he walked along the aisles of his department lie seemed to be sailing on a sea of frangipanni, while white clouds, machine-embroidered, floated around him. Too many sweets bring surfeit. He looked upon Hetty Pepper's homely countenance, emerald eyes, and chocolate-colored hair as a welcome oasis of green in a desert of cloying beauty. In a quiet angle of a counter he pinched her arm kindly, three inches above the elbow. She slapped him three feet away with one good blow of her muscular and not especially lily-white right. So, now you know why Hetty Pepper came to leave the Biggest Store at thirty minutes' notice, with one dime and a nickel in her purse.

This morning's quotations list the price of rib beef at six cents per (butcher's) pound. But on the day that Hetty was "released" by the B. S. the price was seven and one-half cents. That fact is what makes this story possible. Otherwise,the extra four cents would have -

But the plot of nearly all the good stories in the world is concerned with shorts who were unable to cover; so you can find no fault with this one.

Hetty mounted with her rib beef to her $3.50 third-floor back. One hot, savory beef-stew for supper, a night's good sleep, and she would be fit in the morning to apply again for the tasks of Hercules, Joan of Arc, Una, Job, and Little-Red-Riding-Hood.

In her room she got the granite-ware stew-pan out of the 2x4-foot China – er - I mean earthenware closet, and began to dig down in a rats'-nest of paper bags for the potatoes and onions. She came out with her nose and chin just a little sharper pointed.

There was neither a potato nor an onion. Now, what kind of a beef-Stew can you make out of simply beef? You can make oyster-soup without oysters, turtle-soup without turtles, coffee-cake without coffee, but you can't make beef-stew without potatoes and onions.

But rib beef alone, in an emergency, can make an ordinary pine door look like a wrought-iron gambling-house portal to the wolf. With salt and pepper and a tablespoonful of flour (first well stirred in a little cold water) 'twill serve, 'tis not so deep as a lobster a la Newburg nor so wide as a church festival doughnut; but 'twill serve.

Hetty took her stew-pan to the rear of the third-floor hall.

According to the advertisements of the Vallambrosa there was running water to be found there. Between you and me and the water-meter, it only ambled or walked through the faucets; but technicalities have no place here. There was also a sink where housekeeping roomers often met to dump their coffee grounds and glare at one another's kimonos.

At this sink Hetty found a girl with heavy, gold-brown, artistic hair and plaintive eyes, washing two large "Irish" potatoes. Hetty knew the Vallambrosa as well as anyone not owning "double hextra-magnifying eyes" could compass its mysteries. The kimonos were her encyclopedia, her "Who's What?" her clearinghouse of news, of goers and comers. From a rose-pink kimono edged with Nile green she had learned that the girl with the potatoes was a miniature-painter living in a kind of attic - or "studio," as they prefer to call it, on the top floor. Hetty was not certain in her mind what a miniature was; but it certainly wasn't a house; because house-painters, although they wear splashy overalls and poke ladders in your face on the street, are known to indulge in a riotous profusion of food at home.

The potato girl was quite slim and small, and handled her potatoes as an old bachelor uncle handles a baby who is cutting teeth. She had a dull shoemaker's knife in her right hand, and she had begun to peel one of the potatoes with it.

Hetty addressed her in the punctiliously formal tone of one who intends to be cheerfully familiar with you in the second round.

"Beg pardon," she said, "for butting into what's not my business, but if you peel them potatoes you lose out. They're new Bermudas. You want to scrape 'em. Lemme show you."

She took a potato and the knife, and began to demonstrate.

"Oh, thank you," breathed the artist. "I didn't know. And I did hate to see the thick peeling go; it seemed such a waste. But I thought they always had to be peeled. When you've got only potatoes to eat, the peelings count, you know."

"Say, kid," said Hetty, staying her knife, "you ain't up against it, too, are you?"

The miniature artist smiled starvedly.

"I suppose I am. Art, or, at least, the way I interpret it, doesn't seem to be much in demand. I have only these potatoes for my dinner. But they aren't so bad boiled and hot, with a little butter and salt."

"Child," said Hetty, letting a brief smile soften her rigid features, "Fate has sent me and you together. I've had it handed to me in the neck, too; but I've got a chunk of meat in my, room as big as a lap-dog. And I've done everything to get potatoes except pray for 'em.

Let's me and you bunch our commissary departments and make a stew of 'em.

We'll cook it in my room. If we only had an onion to go in it!
Say, kid, you haven't got a couple of pennies that've slipped down into the lining of your last winter's sealskin, have you? I could step down to the corner and get one at old Giuseppe's stand. A stew without an onion is worse'n a matinee without candy."

"You may call me Cecilia," said the artist. "No; I spent my last penny three days ago."

"Then we'll have to cut the onion out instead of slicing it in," said Hetty. "I'd ask the janitress for one, but I don't want 'em hep just yet to the fact that I'm pounding the asphalt for another job. But I wish we did have an onion."

In the shop-girl's room the two began to prepare their supper. Cecilia's part was to sit on the couch helplessly and beg to be allowed to do something, in the voice of a cooing ring-dove. Hetty prepared the rib beef, putting it in cold salted water in the stew-pan and setting it on the one-burner gas-stove.

"I wish we had an onion," said Hetty, as she scraped the two potatoes.

On the wall opposite the couch was pinned a flaming, gorgeous advertising picture of one of the new ferry-boats of the P. U. F. F. Railroad that had been built to cut down the time between Los Angeles and New York City one-eighth of a minute.

Hetty, turning her head during her continuous monologue, saw tears running from her guest's eyes as she gazed on the idealized presentment of the speeding, foam-girdled transport.

"Why, say, Cecilia, kid," said Hetty, poising her knife, "is it as bad art as that? I ain't a critic; but I thought it kind of brightened up the room. Of course, a manicure-painter could tell it was a bum picture in a minute. I'll take it down if you say so. I wish to the holy Saint Potluck we had an onion."

But the miniature miniature-painter had tumbled down, sobbing, with her nose indenting the hard-woven drapery of the couch. Something was here deeper than the artistic temperament offended at crude lithography.

Hetty knew. She had accepted her role long ago. How scant the words with which we try to describe a single quality of a human being! When we reach the abstract we are lost. The nearer to Nature that the babbling of our lips comes, the better do we understand. Figuratively (let us say), some people are Bosoms, some are Hands, some are Heads, some are Muscles, some are Feet, some are Backs for burdens.

Hetty was a Shoulder. Hers was a sharp, sinewy shoulder; but all her life people had laid their heads upon it, metaphorically or actually, and had left there all or half their troubles. Looking at Life anatomically, which is as good a way as any, she was preordained to be a Shoulder. There were few truer collar-bones anywhere than hers.

Hetty was only thirty-three, and she had not yet outlived the little pang that visited her whenever the head of youth and beauty leaned upon her for consolation. But one glance in her mirror always served as an instantaneous pain-killer. So she gave one pale look into the crinkly old looking-glass on the wall above the gas-stove, turned down the flame a little lower from the bubbling beef and potatoes, went over to the couch, and lifted Cecilia's head to its confessional.

"Go on and tell me, honey," she said. "I know now that it ain't art that's worrying you. You met him on a ferry-boat, didn't you? Go on, Cecilia, kid, and tell your, your Aunt Hetty about it."

But youth and melancholy must first spend the surplus of sighs and tears that waft and float the barque of romance to its harbor in the delectable isles. Presently, through the stringy tendons that formed the bars of the confessional, the penitent or was it the glorified communicant of the sacred flame, told her story without art or illumination.

"It was only three days ago. I was coming back on the ferry from Jersey City. Old Mr. Schrum, an art dealer, told me of a rich man in Newark who wanted a miniature of his daughter painted. I went to see him and showed him some of my work. When I told him the price would be fifty dollars he laughed at me like a hyena. He said an enlarged crayon twenty times the size would cost him only eight dollars.

"I had just enough money to buy my ferry ticket back to New York. I felt as if I didn't want to live another day. I must have looked as I felt, for I saw him on the row of seats opposite me, looking at me as if he understood. He was nice-looking, but oh, above everything else, he looked kind. When one is tired or unhappy or hopeless, kindness counts more than anything else.

"When I got so miserable that I couldn't fight against it any longer, I got up and walked slowly out the rear door of the ferry-boat cabin. No one was there, and I slipped quickly over the rail and dropped into the water. Oh, friend Hetty, it was cold, cold!

"For just one moment I wished I was back in the old Vallambrosa,
starving and hoping. And then I got numb, and didn't care. And then
I felt that somebody else was in the water close by me, holding me up.
He had followed me, and jumped in to save me.

"Somebody threw a thing like a big, white doughnut at us, and he made
me put my arms through the hole. Then the ferry-boat backed, and they
pulled us on board. Oh, Hetty, I was so ashamed of my wickedness in
trying to drown myself; and, besides, my hair had all tumbled down and
was sopping wet, and I was such a sight.

"And then some men in blue clothes came around; and he gave them his
card, and I heard him tell them he had seen me drop my purse on the
edge of the boat outside the rail, and in leaning over to get it I had
fallen overboard.

And then I remembered having read in the papers that people who try to
kill themselves are locked up in cells with people who try to kill
other people, and I was afraid.

"But some ladies on the boat took me downstairs to the furnace-room
and got me nearly dry and did up my hair. When the boat landed, he
came and put me in a cab. He was all dripping himself, but laughed as
if he thought it was all a joke. He begged me, but I wouldn't tell
him my name nor where I lived, I was so ashamed."

"You were a fool, child," said Hetty, kindly. "Wait till I turn the light
up a bit. I wish to Heaven we had an onion."

"Then he raised his hat," went on Cecilia, "and said: 'Very well. But
I'll find you, anyhow. I'm going to claim my rights of salvage.' Then
he gave money to the cab-driver and told him to take me where I
wanted to go, and walked away. What is 'salvage,' Hetty?"

"The edge of a piece of goods that ain't hemmed," said the shop-girl.
"You must have looked pretty well frazzled out to the little hero boy."

"It's been three days," moaned the miniature-painter, "and he hasn't
found me yet."

"Extend the time," said Hetty. "This is a big town. Think of how
many girls he might have to see soaked in water with their hair down
before he would recognize you. The stew's getting on fine but oh,
for an onion! I'd even use a piece'of garlic if I had it."

The beef and potatoes bubbled merrily, exhaling a mouth-watering savor that yet lacked something, leaving a hunger on the palate, a haunting, wistful desire for some lost and needful ingredient.

"I came near drowning in that awful river," said Cecilia, shuddering.

"It ought to have more water in it," said Hetty; "the stew, I mean. I'll go get some at the sink."

"It smells good," said the artist.

"That nasty old North River?" objected Hetty. "It smells to me like soap factories and wet setter-dogs, oh, you mean the stew. Well, I wish we had an onion for it. Did he look like he had money?"

"First, he looked kind," said Cecilia. "I'm sure he was rich; but that matters so little. When he drew out his bill-folder to pay the cab-man you couldn't help seeing hundreds and thousands of dollars in it. And I looked over the cab doors and saw him leave the ferry station in a motor-car; and the chauffeur gave him his bearskin to put on, for he was sopping wet. And it was only three days ago."

"What a fool!" said Hetty, shortly.

"Oh, the chauffeur wasn't wet," breathed Cecilia. "And he drove the car away very nicely."

"I mean you," said Hetty. "For not giving him your address."

"I never give my address to chauffeurs," said Cecilia, haughtily.

"I wish we had one," said Hetty, disconsolately.

"What for?"

"For the stew, of course, oh, I mean an onion."

Hetty took a pitcher and started to the sink at the end of the hall.

A young man came down the stairs from above just as she was opposite the lower step. He was decently dressed, but pale and haggard. His eyes were dull with the stress of some burden of physical or mental woe. In his hand he bore an onion, a pink, smooth, solid, shining onion as large around as a ninety-eight-cent alarm-clock.

Hetty stopped. So did the young man. There was something Joan of

Arc-ish, Herculean, and Una-ish in the look and pose of the shoplady, she
had cast off the roles of Job and Little-Red-Riding-Hood. The
young man stopped at the foot of the stairs and coughed distractedly.
He felt marooned, held up, attacked, assailed, levied upon, sacked,
assessed, panhandled, browbeaten, though he knew not why. It was the
look in Hetty's eyes that did it. In them he saw the Jolly Roger fly
to the masthead and an able seaman with a dirk between his teeth
scurry up the ratlines and nail it there. But as yet he did not know
that the cargo he carried was the thing that had caused him to be so
nearly blown out of the water without even a parley.

"Beg your pardon," said Hetty, as sweetly as her dilute acetic acid
tones permitted, "but did you find that onion on the stairs? There
was a hole in the paper bag; and I've just come out to look for it."

The young man coughed for half a minute. The interval may have given
him the courage to defend his own property. Also, he clutched his
pungent prize greedily, and, with a show of spirit, faced his grim
waylayer.

"No," he said huskily, "I didn't find it on the stairs. It was given
to me by Jack Bevens, on the top floor. If you don't believe it, ask
him. I'll wait until you do."

"I know about Bevens," said Hetty, sourly. "He writes books and
things up there for the paper-and-rags man. We can hear the postman
guy him all over the house when he brings them thick envelopes back.
Say, do you live in the Vallambrosa?"

"I do not," said the young man. "I come to see Bevens sometimes.
He's my friend. I live two blocks west."

"What are you going to do with the onion? begging your pardon," said
Hetty.

"I'm going to eat it."

"Raw?"

"Yes: as soon as I get home."

"Haven't you got anything else to eat with it?"

The young man considered briefly.

"No," he confessed; "there's not another scrap of anything in my
diggings to eat. I think old Jack is pretty hard up for grub in his

shack, too. He hated to give up the onion, but I worried him into parting with it."

"Man," said Hetty, fixing him with her world-sapient eyes, and laying a bony but impressive finger on his sleeve, "you've known trouble, too, haven't you?"

"Lots," said the onion owner, promptly. "But this onion is my own property, honestly come by. If you will excuse me, I must be going."

"Listen," said Hetty, paling a little with anxiety. "Raw onion is a mighty poor diet. And so is a beef-stew without one. Now, if you're Jack Bevens' friend, I guess you're nearly right. There's a little Lady, a friend of mine, in my room there at the end of the hall. Both of us are out of luck; and we had just potatoes and meat between us. They're stewing now. But it ain't got any soul. There's something lacking to it. There's certain things in life that are naturally intended to fit and belong together. One is pink cheese-cloth and green roses, and one is ham and eggs, and one is Irish and trouble. And the other one is beef and potatoes with onions. And still another one is people who are up against it and other people in the same fix."

The young man went into a protracted paroxysm of coughing. With one hand he hugged his onion to his bosom.

"No doubt; no doubt," said he, at length. "But, as I said, I must be going, because -"

Hetty clutched his sleeve firmly.

"Don't be a Dago, Little Brother. Don't cat raw onions. Chip it in toward the dinner and line yourself inside with the best stew you ever licked a spoon over. Must two ladies knock a young gentleman down and drag him inside for the honor of dining with 'em? No harm shall befall you, Little Brother. Loosen up and fall into line."

The young man's pale face relaxed into a grin.

"Believe I'll go you," he said, brightening. "If my onion is good as a credential, I'll accept the invitation gladly."

"It's good as that, but better as seasoning," said Hetty. "You come and stand outside the door till I ask my lady friend if she has any objections. And don't run away with that letter of recommendation before I come out."

Hetty went into her room and closed the door. The young man waited outside.

"Cecilia, kid," said the shop-girl, oiling the sharp saw of her voice as well as she could, "there's an onion outside. With a young man attached. I've asked him in to dinner. You ain't going to kick, are you?"

"Oh, dear!" said Cecilia, sitting up and patting her artistic hair. She cast a mournful glance at the ferry-boat poster on the wall.

"Nit," said Hetty. "It ain't him. You're up against real life now. I believe you said your hero friend had money and automobiles. This is a poor skeezicks that's got nothing to eat but an onion. But he's easy-spoken and not a freshy. I imagine he's been a gentleman, he's so low down now. And we need the onion. Shall I bring him in? I'll guarantee his behavior."

"Hetty, dear," sighed Cecilia, "I'm so hungry. What difference does it make whether he's a prince or a burglar? I don't care. Bring him in if he's got anything to eat with him."

Hetty went back into the hall. The onion man was gone. Her heart missed a beat, and a gray look settled over her face except on her nose and cheek-bones. And then the tides of life flowed in again, for she saw him leaning out of the front window at the other end of the hall. She hurried there. He was shouting to some one below. The noise of the street overpowered the sound of her footsteps. She looked down over his shoulder, saw whom he was speaking to, and heard his words. He pulled himself in from the window-sill and saw her standing over him.

Hetty's eyes bored into him like two steel gimlets.

"Don't lie to me," she said, calmly. "What were you going to do with that onion?"

The young man suppressed a cough and faced her resolutely. His manner was that of one who had been bearded sufficiently.

"I was going to eat it," said he, with emphatic slowness; "just as I told you before."

"And you have nothing else to eat at home?"

"Not a thing."

"What kind of work do you do?"

"I am not working at anything just now."

"Then why," said Hetty, with her voice set on its sharpest edge, "do you lean out of windows and give orders to chauffeurs in green automobiles in the street below?"

The young man flushed, and his dull eyes began to sparkle.

"Because, madam," said he, in accelerando tones, "I pay the chauffeur's wages and I own the automobile and also this onion - this onion, madam."

He flourished the onion within an inch of Hetty's nose. The shop-lady did not retreat a hair's-breadth.

"Then why do you eat onions," she said, with biting contempt, "and nothing else?"

"I never said I did," retorted the young man, heatedly. "I said I had nothing else to eat where I live. I am not a delicatessen store keeper."

"Then why," pursued Hetty, inflexibly, "were you going to eat a raw onion?"

"My mother," said the young man, "always made me eat one for a cold. Pardon my referring to a physical infirmity; but you may have noticed that I have a very, very severe cold. I was going to eat the onion and go to bed. I wonder why I am standing here and apologizing to you for it."

"How did you catch this cold?" went on Hetty, suspiciously.

The young man seemed to have arrived at some extreme height of feeling. There were two modes of descent open to him, a burst of rage or a surrender to the ridiculous. He chose wisely; and the empty hall echoed his hoarse laughter.

"You're a dandy," said he. "And I don't blame you for being careful. I don't mind telling you. I got wet. I was on a North River ferry a few days ago when a girl jumped overboard. Of course, I -"

Hetty extended her hand, interrupting his story.

"Give me the onion," she said.

The young man set his jaw a trifle harder.

"Give me the onion," she repeated.

He grinned, and laid it in her hand.

Then Hetty's infrequent, grim, melancholy smile showed itself. She took the young man's arm and pointed with her other hand to the door of her room.

"Little Brother," she said, "go in there. The little fool you fished out of the river is there waiting for you. Go on in. I'll give you three minutes before I come. Potatoes is in there, waiting. Go on in, Onions."

After he had tapped at the door and entered, Hetty began to peel and wash the onion at the sink. She gave a gray look at the gray roofs outside, and the smile on her face vanished by little jerks and twitches.

"But it's us," she said, grimly, to herself, "it's us that furnishes the beef."

THE HIDING OF BLACK BILL

A lank, strong, red-faced man with a Wellington beak and small, fiery eyes tempered by flaxen lashes, sat on the station platform at Los Pinos swinging his legs to and fro. At his side sat another man, fat, melancholy, and seedy, who seemed to be his friend. They had the appearance of men to whom life had appeared as a reversible coat, seamy on both sides.

"Ain't seen you in about four years, Ham," said the seedy man. "Which way you been travelling?"

"Texas," said the red-faced man. "It was too cold in Alaska for me. And I found it warm in Texas. I'll tell you about one hot spell I went through there.

"One morning I steps off the International at a water-tank and lets it go on without me. 'Twas a ranch country, and fuller of spite-houses than New York City. Only out there they build 'em twenty miles away so you can't smell what they've got for dinner, instead of running 'em up two inches from their neighbors' windows.

"There wasn't any roads in sight, so I footed it 'cross country. The grass was shoe-top deep, and the mesquite timber looked just like a peach orchard. It was so much like a gentleman's private estate that every minute you expected a kennelful of bulldogs to run out and bite you. But I must have walked twenty miles before I came in sight of a ranch-house. It was a little one, about as big as an elevated railroad station.

"There was a little man in a white shirt and brown overalls and a pink handkerchief around his neck rolling cigarettes under a tree in front of the door.

"'Greetings,' says I. 'Any refreshment, welcome, emoluments, or even work for a comparative stranger?'

"'Oh, come in,' says he, in a refined tone. 'Sit down on that stool, please. I didn't hear your horse coming.'

"'He isn't near enough yet,' says I. 'I walked. I don't want to be a burden, but I wonder if you have three or four gallons of water handy.'

"'You do look pretty dusty,' says he; 'but our bathing arrangements -'

"'It's a drink I want,' says I. 'Never mind the dust that's on the outside.'

"He gets me a dipper of water out of a red jar hanging up, and then goes on:

"'Do you want work?'

"'For a time,' says I. 'This is a rather quiet section of the country, isn't it?'

"'It is,' says he. 'Sometimes, so I have been told, one sees no human being pass for weeks at a time. I've been here only a month. I bought the ranch from an old settler who wanted to move farther west.'

"'It suits me,' says I. 'Quiet and retirement are good for a man sometimes. And I need a job. I can tend bar, salt mines, lecture, float stock, do a little middle-weight slugging, and play the piano.'

"'Can you herd sheep?' asks the little ranch-man.

"'Do you mean have I heard sheep?' says I.

"'Can you herd 'em, take charge of a flock of 'em ?' says he.

"'Oh,' says I, 'now I understand. You mean chase 'em around and bark at 'em like collie dogs. Well, I might,' says I. 'I've never exactly done any sheep-herding, but I've often seen 'em from car windows masticating daisies, and they don't look dangerous.'

"'I'm short a herder,' says the ranchman. 'You never can depend on the Mexicans. I've only got two flocks. You may take out my bunch of muttons, there are only eight hundred of 'em, in the morning, if you like. The pay is twelve dollars a month and your rations furnished. You camp in a tent on the prairie with your sheep. You do your own cooking, but wood and water are brought to your camp. It's an easy job.'

"'I'm on,' says I. 'I'll take the job even if I have to garland my brow and hold on to a crook and wear a loose-effect and play on a pipe like the shepherds do in pictures.'

"So the next morning the little ranchman helps me drive the flock of muttons from the corral to about two miles out and let 'em graze on a little hillside on the prairie. He gives me a lot of instructions about not letting bunches of them stray off from the herd, and driving 'em down to a water-hole to drink at noon.

"'I'll bring out your tent and camping outfit and rations in the buckboard before night,' says he.

"'Fine,' says I. 'And don't forget the rations. Nor the camping outfit. And be sure to bring the tent. Your name's Zollicoffer, ain't it?"

"'My name,' says he, 'is Henry Ogden.'

"'All right, Mr. Ogden,' says I. 'Mine is Mr. Percival Saint Clair.'

"I herded sheep for five days on the Rancho Chiquito; and then the wool entered my soul. That getting next to Nature certainly got next to me. I was lonesomer than Crusoe's goat. I've seen a lot of persons more entertaining as companions than those sheep were. I'd drive 'em to the corral and pen 'em every evening, and then cook my corn-bread and mutton and coffee, and lie down in a tent the size of a table-cloth, and listen to the coyotes and whippoorwills singing around the camp.

"The fifth evening, after I had corralled my costly but uncongenial muttons, I walked over to the ranch-house and stepped in the door.

"'Mr. Ogden,' says I, 'you and me have got to get sociable. Sheep are all very well to dot the landscape and furnish eight-dollar cotton suitings for man, but for table-talk and fireside companions they rank along with five-o'clock teazers. If you've got a deck of cards, or a parcheesi outfit, or a game of authors, get 'em out, and let's get on a mental basis. I've got to do something in an intellectual line, if it's only to knock somebody's brains out.'

"This Henry Ogden was a peculiar kind of ranchman. He wore finger-rings and a big gold watch and careful neckties. And his face was calm, and his nose-spectacles was kept very shiny. I saw once, in Muscogee, an outlaw hung for murdering six men, who was a dead ringer for him. But I knew a preacher in Arkansas that you would have taken to be his brother. I didn't care much for him either way; what I wanted was some fellowship and communion with holy saints or lost sinners, anything sheepless would do.

"'Well, Saint Clair,' says he, laying down the book he was reading, 'I guess it must be pretty lonesome for you at first. And I don't deny that it's monotonous for me. Are you sure you corralled your sheep so they won't stray out ?

"'They're shut up as tight as the jury of a millionaire murderer,' says I. 'And I'll be back with them long before they'll need their trained nurse.'

"So Ogden digs up a deck of cards, and we play casino. After five days and nights of my sheep-camp it was like a toot on Broadway. When I caught big casino I felt as excited as if I had made a million in Trinity. And when H. O. loosened up a little and told the story about the lady in the Pullman car I laughed for five minutes.

"That showed what a comparative thing life is. A man may see so much that he'd be bored to turn his head to look at a $3,000,000 fire or Joe Weber or the Adriatic Sea. But let him herd sheep for a spell, and you'll see him splitting his ribs laughing at 'Curfew Shall Not Ring To-night,' or really enjoying himself playing cards with ladies.

"By-and-by Ogden gets out a decanter of Bourbon, and then there is a total eclipse of sheep.

"'Do you remember reading in the papers, about a month ago,' says he, 'about a train hold-up on the M. K. & T.? The express agent was shot through the shoulder, and about $15,000 in currency taken. And it's said that only one man did the job.'

"'Seems to me I do,' says I. 'But such things happen so often they don't linger long in the human Texas mind. Did they overtake, overhaul, seize, or lay hands upon the despoiler?'

"'He escaped,' says Ogden. 'And I was just reading in a paper to-day that the officers have tracked him down into this part of the country. It seems the bills the robber got were all the first issue of currency to the Second National Bank of Espinosa City. And so they've followed the trail where they've been spent, and it leads this way.'

"Ogden pours out some more Bourbon, and shoves me the bottle.

"'I imagine,' says I, after ingurgitating another modicum of the royal boose, 'that it wouldn't be at all a disingenuous idea for a train robber to run down into this part of the country to hide for a spell. A sheep-ranch, now,' says I, would be the finest kind of a place. Who'd ever expect to find such a desperate character among these song-birds and muttons and wild flowers? And, by the way,' says I, kind of looking H. Ogden over, 'was there any description mentioned of this single-handed terror? Was his lineaments or height and thickness or teeth fillings or style of habiliments set forth in print ?'

"'Why, no,' says Ogden; 'they say nobody got a good sight of him because he wore a mask. But they know it was a train-robber called Black Bill, because he always works alone and because he dropped a handkerchief in the express-car that had his name on it.'

"'All right,' says I. 'I approve of Black Bill's retreat to the sheep ranges. I guess they won't find him.'

"'There's one thousand dollars reward for his capture,' says Ogden.

"'I don't need that kind of money,' says I, looking Mr. Sheepman straight in the eye. 'The twelve dollars a month you pay me is enough. I need a rest, and I can save up until I get enough to pay my fare to Texarkana, where my widowed mother lives. If Black Bill,' I goes on, looking significantly at Ogden, was to have come down this way, say, a month ago and bought a little sheep-ranch and -'

"'Stop,' says Ogden, getting out of his chair and looking pretty vicious. 'Do you mean to insinuate -'

"'Nothing,' says I; 'no insinuations. I'm stating a hypodermical case. I say, if Black Bill had come down here and bought a sheep-ranch and hired me to Little-Boy-Blue 'em and treated me square and friendly, as you've done, he'd never have anything to fear from me. A man is a man, regardless of any complications he may have with sheep or railroad trains. Now you know where I stand.'

"Ogden looks black as camp-coffee for nine seconds, and then he laughs, amused.

"'You'll do, Saint Clair,' says he. 'If I was Black Bill I wouldn't
be afraid to trust you. Let's have a game or two of seven-up to-
night. That is, if you don't mind playing with a train-robber.'

"'I've told you,' says I, 'my oral sentiments, and there's no strings
to 'em.'

"While I was shuffling after the first hand, I asks Ogden, as if the
idea was a kind of a casualty, where he was from.

"'Oh,' says he, 'from the Mississippi Valley.'

"'That's a nice little place,' says I. 'I've often stopped over there.
But didn't you find the sheets a little damp and the food poor? Now,
I hail,' says I, 'from the Pacific Slope. Ever put up there?'

"'Too draughty,' says Ogden. 'But if you've ever in the Middle West
just mention my name, and you'll get foot-warmers and dripped coffee.'

"'Well,' says I, 'I wasn't exactly fishing for your private telephone
number and the middle name of your aunt that carried off the
Cumberland Presbyterian minister. It don't matter. I just want you
to know you are safe in the hands of your shepherd. Now, don't play
hearts on spades, and don't get nervous.'

"'Still harping,' says Ogden, laughing again. 'Don't you suppose that
if I was Black Bill and thought you suspected me, I'd put a Winchester
bullet into you and stop my nervousness, if I had any?'

"'Not any,' says I. 'A man who's got the nerve to hold up a train
single-handed wouldn't do a trick like that. I've knocked about
enough to know that them are the kind of men who put a value on a
friend. Not that I can claim being a friend of yours, Mr. Ogden,'
says I, 'being only your sheep-herder; but under more expeditious
circumstances we might have been.'

"'Forget the sheep temporarily, I beg,' says Ogden, 'and cut for
deal.'

"About four days afterward, while my muttons was nooning on the water-
hole and I deep in the interstices of making a pot of coffee, up rides
softly on the grass a mysterious person in the garb of the being he
wished to represent. He was dressed somewhere between a Kansas City
detective, Buffalo Bill, and the town dog-catcher of Baton Rouge. His
chin and eye wasn't molded on fighting lines, so I knew he was only a

scout.

"'Herdin' sheep?' he asks me.

"'Well,' says I, 'to a man of your evident gumptional endowments, I wouldn't have the nerve to state that I am engaged in decorating old bronzes or oiling bicycle sprockets.'

"'You don't talk or look like a sheep-herder to me,' says he.

"'But you talk like what you look like to me,' says I.

"And then he asks me who I was working for, and I shows him Rancho Chiquito, two miles away, in the shadow of a low hill, and he tells me he's a deputy sheriff.

"'There's a train-robber called Black Bill supposed to be somewhere in these parts,' says the scout. 'He's been traced as far as San Antonio, and maybe farther. Have you seen or heard of any strangers around here during the past month?'

"'I have not,' says I, 'except a report of one over at the Mexican quarters of Loomis' ranch, on the Frio.'

"'What do you know about him?' asks the deputy.

"'He's three days old,' says I.

"'What kind of a looking man is the man you work for ?' he asks. 'Does old George Ramey own this place yet? He's run sheep here for the last ten years, but never had no success.'

"'The old man has sold out and gone West,' I tells him. 'Another sheep-fancier bought him out about a month ago.'

"'What kind of a looking man is he ?' asks the deputy again.

"'Oh,' says I, ' a big, fat kind of a Dutchman with long whiskers and blue specs. I don't think he knows a sheep from a ground-squirrel. I guess old George soaked him pretty well on the deal,' says I.

"After indulging himself in a lot more non-communicative information and two-thirds of my dinner, the deputy rides away.

"That night I mentions the matter to Ogden. "'They're drawing the tendrils of the octopus around Black Bill,' says I. And then I told him about the deputy sheriff, and how I'd described him to the deputy, and what the deputy said about the matter.

"'Oh, well,' says Ogden, 'let's don't borrow any of Black Bill's troubles. We've a few of our own. Get the Bourbon out of the cupboard and we'll drink to his health, unless,' says he, with his little cackling laugh, 'you're prejudiced against train-robbers.'

"'I'll drink,' says I, 'to any man who's a friend to a friend. And I believe that Black Bill,' I goes on, 'would be that. So here's to Black Bill, and may he have good luck.'

"And both of us drank.

"About two weeks later comes shearing-time. The sheep had to be driven up to the ranch, and a lot of frowzy-headed Mexicans would snip the fur off of them with back-action scissors. So the afternoon before the barbers were to come I hustled my underdone muttons over the hill, across the dell, down by the winding brook, and up to the ranch-house, where I penned 'em in a corral and bade 'em my nightly adieus.

"I went from there to the ranch-house. I find H. Ogden, Esquire, lying asleep on his little cot bed. I guess he had been overcome by anti-insomnia or diswakefulness or some of the diseases peculiar to the sheep business. His mouth and vest were open, and he breathed like a second-hand bicycle pump. I looked at him and gave vent to just a few musings. 'Imperial Caesar,' says I, 'asleep in such a way, might shut his mouth and keep the wind away.'

A man asleep is certainly a sight to make angels weep. What good is all his brain, muscle, backing, nerve, influence, and family connections? He's at the mercy of his enemies, and more so of his friends. And he's about as beautiful as a cab-horse leaning against the Metropolitan Opera House at 12.30 A.M. dreaming of the plains of Arabia. Now, a woman asleep you regard as different. No matter how she looks, you know it's better for all hands for her to be that way.

"Well, I took a drink of Bourbon and one for Ogden, and started in to be comfortable while he was taking his nap. He had some books on his table on indigenous subjects, such as Japan and drainage and physical culture, and some tobacco, which seemed more to the point.

"After I'd smoked a few, and listened to the sartorial breathing of H. O., I happened to look out the window toward the shearing-pens, where there was a kind of a road coming up from a kind of a road across a kind of a creek farther away.

"I saw five men riding up to the house. All of 'em carried guns
across their saddles, and among 'em was the deputy that had talked to
me at my camp.

"They rode up careful, in open formation, with their guns ready. I
set apart with my eye the one I opinionated to be the boss muck-raker
of this law-and-order cavalry.

"'Good-evening, gents,' says I. 'Won't you 'light, and tie your horses?'

"The boss rides up close, and swings his gun over till the opening in
it seems to cover my whole front elevation.

"'Don't you move your hands none,' says he, 'till you and me indulge
in a adequate amount of necessary conversation.'

"'I will not,' says I. 'I am no deaf-mute, and therefore will not have to
disobey your injunctions in replying.'

"'We are on the lookout,' says he, 'for Black Bill, the man that held
up the Katy for $15,000 in May. We are searching the ranches and
everybody on 'em. What is your name, and what do you do on this
ranch?'

"'Captain,' says I, 'Percival Saint Clair is my occupation, and my
name is sheep-herder. I've got my flock of veals - no, muttons - penned
here to-night. The shearers are coming to-morrow to give them a hair-
cut - with baa-a-rum, I suppose.'

"'Where's the boss of this ranch?' the captain of the gang asks me.

"'Wait just a minute, cap'n,' says I. 'Wasn't there a kind of a
reward offered for the capture of this desperate character you have
referred to in your preamble?'

"'There's a thousand dollars reward offered,' says the captain, 'but
it's for his capture and conviction. There don't seem to be no
provision made for an informer.'

"'It looks like it might rain in a day or so,' says I, in a tired way,
looking up at the cerulean blue sky.

"'If you know anything about the locality, disposition, or
secretiveness of this here Black Bill,' says he, in a severe dialect,
'you are amiable to the law in not reporting it.'

"'I heard a fence-rider say,' says I, in a desultory kind of voice, 'that a Mexican told a cowboy named Jake over at Pidgin's store on the Nueces that he heard that Black Bill had been seen in Matamoras by a sheepman's cousin two weeks ago.'

"'Tell you what I'll do, Tight Mouth,' says the captain, after looking me over for bargains. 'If you put us on so we can scoop Black Bill, I'll pay you a hundred dollars out of my own - out of our own - pockets. That's liberal,' says he. 'You ain't entitled to anything. Now, what do you say?'

"'Cash down now?' I asks.

"The captain has a sort of discussion with his helpmates, and they all produce the contents of their pockets for analysis. Out of the general results they figured up $102.30 in cash and $31 worth of plug tobacco.

"'Come nearer, capitan meeo,' says I, 'and listen.' He so did.

"'I am mighty poor and low down in the world,' says I. 'I am working for twelve dollars a month trying to keep a lot of animals together whose only thought seems to be to get asunder. Although,' says I, 'I regard myself as some better than the State of South Dakota, it's a come-down to a man who has heretofore regarded sheep only in the form of chops. I'm pretty far reduced in the world on account of foiled ambitions and rum and a kind of cocktail they make along the P. R. R. all the way from Scranton to Cincinnati; dry gin, French vermouth, one squeeze of a lime, and a good dash of orange bitters. If you're ever up that way, don't fail to let one try you. And, again,' says I, 'I have never yet went back on a friend. I've stayed by 'em when they had plenty, and when adversity's overtaken me I've never forsook 'em.

"'But,' I goes on, 'this is not exactly the case of a friend. Twelve dollars a month is only bowing-acquaintance money. And I do not consider brown beans and corn-bread the food of friendship. I am a poor man,' says I, 'and I have a widowed mother in Texarkana. You will find Black Bill,' says I, 'lying asleep in this house on a cot in the room to your right. He's the man you want, as I know from his words and conversation. He was in a way a friend,' I explains, 'and if I was the man I once was the entire product of the mines of Gondola would not have tempted me to betray him. But,' says I, 'every week half of the beans was wormy, and not nigh enough wood in camp.

"'Better go in careful, gentlemen,' says I. 'He seems impatient at times, and when you think of his late professional pursuits one would look for abrupt actions if he was come upon sudden.'

"So the whole posse unmounts and ties their horses, and unlimbers their ammunition and equipments, and tiptoes into the house. And I follows, like Delilah when she set the Philip Stein on to Samson.

"The leader of the posse shakes Ogden and wakes him up. And then he jumps up, and two more of the reward-hunters grab him. Ogden was mighty tough with all his slimness, and he gives 'em as neat a single-footed tussle against odds as I ever see.

"'What does this mean?' he says, after they had him down.

"'You're scooped in, Mr. Black Bill,' says the captain. 'That's all.'

"'It's an outrage,' says H. Ogden, madder yet.

"'It was,' says the peace-and-good-will man. 'The Katy wasn't bothering you, and there's a law against monkeying with express packages.'

"And he sits on H. Ogden's stomach and goes through his pockets symptomatically and careful.

"'I'll make you perspire for this,' says Ogden, perspiring some himself. 'I can prove who I am.'

"'So can I,' says the captain, as he draws from H. Ogden's inside coat-pocket a handful of new bills of the Second National Bank of Espinosa City. 'Your regular engraved Tuesdays-and-Fridays visiting-card wouldn't have a louder voice in proclaiming your indemnity than this here currency. You can get up now and prepare to go with us and expatriate your sins.

"H. Ogden gets up and fixes his necktie. He says no more after they have taken the money off of him.

"'A well-greased idea,' says the sheriff captain, admiring, 'to slip off down here and buy a little sheep-ranch where the hand of man is seldom heard. It was the slickest hide-out I ever see,' says the captain.

"So one of the men goes to the shearing-pen and hunts up the other herder, a Mexican they call John Sallies, and he saddles Ogden's horse, and the sheriffs all ride tip close around him with their guns in hand, ready to take their prisoner to town.

"Before starting, Ogden puts the ranch in John Sallies' hands and gives him orders about the shearing and where to graze the sheep, just as if he intended to be back in a few days. And a couple of hours afterward one Percival Saint Clair, an ex-sheep-herder of the Rancho Chiquito, might have been seen, with a hundred and nine dollars, wages and blood-money, in his pocket, riding south on another horse belonging to said ranch."

The red-faced man paused and listened. The whistle of a coming freight-train sounded far away among the low hills.

The fat, seedy man at his side sniffed, and shook his frowzy head slowly and disparagingly.

"What is it, Snipy?" asked the other. "Got the blues again?"

"No, I ain't" said the seedy one, sniffing again. "But I don't like your talk. You and me have been friends, off and on, for fifteen year; and I never yet knew or heard of you giving anybody up to the law, not no one. And here was a man whose saleratus you had et and at whose table you had played games of cards, if casino can be so called. And yet you inform him to the law and take money for it. It never was like you, I say."

"This H. Ogden," resumed the red-faced man, "through a lawyer, proved himself free by alibis and other legal terminalities, as I so heard afterward. He never suffered no harm. He did me favors, and I hated to hand him over."

"How about the bills they found in his pocket?" asked the seedy man.

"I put 'em there," said the red-faced man, "while he was asleep, when I saw the posse riding up. I was Black Bill. Look out, Snipy, here she comes! We'll board her on the bumpers when she takes water at the tank."

SCHOOLS AND SCHOOLS

I

Old Jerome Warren lived in a hundred-thousand-dollar house at 35 East Fifty-Soforth Street. He was a down-town broker, so rich that he could afford to walk, for his health, a few blocks in the direction of his office every morning, and then call a cab.

He had an adopted son, the son of an old friend named Gilbert - Cyril Scott could play him nicely, who was becoming a successful painter as fast as he could squeeze the paint out of his tubes. Another member of the household was Barbara Ross, a stepniece. Man is born to trouble; so, as old Jerome had no family of his own, he took up the burdens of others.

Gilbert and Barbara got along swimmingly. There was a tacit and tactical understanding all round that the two would stand up under a floral bell some high noon, and promise the minister to keep old Jerome's money in a state of high commotion. But at this point complications must be introduced.

Thirty years before, when old Jerome was young Jerome, there was a brother of his named Dick. Dick went West to seek his or somebody else's fortune. Nothing was heard of him until one day old Jerome had a letter from his brother. It was badly written on ruled paper that smelled of salt bacon and coffee-grounds. The writing was asthmatic and the spelling St. Vitusy.

It appeared that instead of Dick having forced Fortune to stand and deliver, he had been held up himself, and made to give hostages to the enemy. That is, as his letter disclosed, he was on the point of pegging out with a complication of disorders that even whiskey had failed to check. All that his thirty years of prospecting had netted him was one daughter, nineteen years old, as per invoice, whom he was shipping East, charges prepaid, for Jerome to clothe, feed, educate, comfort, and cherish for the rest of her natural life or until matrimony should them part.

Old Jerome was a board-walk. Everybody knows that the world is supported by the shoulders of Atlas; and that Atlas stands on a rail-fence; and that the rail-fence is built on a turtle's back. Now, the turtle has to stand on something; and that is a board-walk made of men like old Jerome.

I do not know whether immortality shall accrue to man; but if not so, I would like to know when men like old Jerome get what is due them?

They met Nevada Warren at the station. She was a little girl, deeply sunburned and wholesomely good-looking, with a manner that was frankly
unsophisticated, yet one that not even a cigar-drummer would intrude upon without thinking twice. Looking at her, somehow you would expect to see her in a short skirt and leather leggings, shooting glass balls or taming mustangs. But in her plain white waist and black skirt she sent you guessing again. With an easy exhibition of strength she swung along a heavy valise, which the uniformed porters tried in vain to wrest from her.

"I am sure we shall be the best of friends," said Barbara, pecking at the firm, sunburned cheek.

"I hope so," said Nevada.

"Dear little niece," said old Jerome, "you are as welcome to my home as if it were your father's own."

"Thanks," said Nevada.

"And I am going to call you 'cousin,'" said Gilbert, with his charming smile.

"Take the valise, please," said Nevada. "It weighs a million pounds. It's got samples from six of dad's old mines in it," she explained to Barbara. "I calculate they'd assay about nine cents to the thousand tons, but I promised him to bring them along."

II

It is a common custom to refer to the usual complication between one man and two ladies, or one lady and two men, or a lady and a man and a nobleman, or - well, any of those problems - as the triangle. But they are never unqualified triangles. They are always isosceles, never equilateral. So, upon the coming of Nevada Warren, she and Gilbert and Barbara Ross lined up into such a figurative triangle; and of that triangle Barbara formed the hypotenuse.

One morning old Jerome was lingering long after breakfast over the dullest morning paper in the city before setting forth to his down-town fly-trap. He had become quite fond of Nevada, finding in her much of his dead brother's quiet independence and unsuspicious frankness.

A maid brought in a note for Miss Nevada Warren.

"A messenger-boy delivered it at the door, please," she said. "He's waiting for an answer."

Nevada, who was whistling a Spanish waltz between her teeth, and watching the carriages and autos roll by in the street, took the envelope. She knew it was from Gilbert, before she opened it, by the little gold palette in the upper left-hand corner.

After tearing it open she pored over the contents for a while, absorbedly. Then, with a serious face, she went and stood at her uncle's elbow.

"Uncle Jerome, Gilbert is a nice boy, isn't he?"

"Why, bless the child!" said old Jerome, crackling his paper loudly; "of course he is. I raised him myself."

"He wouldn't write anything to anybody that wasn't exactly, I mean that everybody couldn't know and read, would he?"

"I'd just like to see him try it," said uncle, tearing a handful from his newspaper. "Why, what -"

"Read this note he just sent me, uncle, and see if you think it's all right and proper. You see, I don't know much about city people and their ways."

Old Jerome threw his paper down and set both his feet upon it. He took Gilbert's note and fiercely perused it twice, and then a third time.

"Why, child," said he, "you had me almost excited, although I was sure of that boy. He's a duplicate of his father, and he was a gilt-edged diamond. He only asks if you and Barbara will be ready at four o'clock this afternoon for an automobile drive over to Long Island. I don't see anything to criticise in it except the stationery. I always did hate that shade of blue."

"Would it be all right to go?" asked Nevada, eagerly.

"Yes, yes, yes, child; of course. Why not? Still, it pleases me to see you so careful and candid. Go, by all means."

"I didn't know," said Nevada, demurely. "I thought I'd ask you. Couldn't you go with us, uncle?"

"I? No, no, no, no! I've ridden once in a car that boy was driving. Never again! But it's entirely proper for you and Barbara to go. Yes, yes. But I will not. No, no, no, no!"

Nevada flew to the door, and said to the maid:

"You bet we'll go. I'll answer for Miss Barbara. Tell the boy to say to Mr. Warren, 'You bet we'll go.'"

"Nevada," called old Jerome, "pardon me, my dear, but wouldn't it be as well to send him a note in reply? Just a line would do."

"No, I won't bother about that," said Nevada, gayly. "Gilbert will Understand, he always does. I never rode in an automobile in my life;

but I've paddled a canoe down Little Devil River through the Lost Horse Canon, and if it's any livelier than that I'd like to know!"

III
Two months are supposed to have elapsed.

Barbara sat in the study of the hundred-thousand-dollar house. It was a good place for her. Many places are provided in the world where men and women may repair for the purpose of extricating themselves from divers difficulties. There are cloisters, wailing-places, watering-places, confessionals, hermitages, lawyer's offices, beauty parlors, air-ships, and studies; and the greatest of these are studies.

It usually takes a hypotenuse a long time to discover that it is the longest side of a triangle. But it's a long line that has no turning.

Barbara was alone. Uncle Jerome and Nevada had gone to the theatre. Barbara had not cared to go. She wanted to stay at home and study in the study. If you, miss, were a stunning New York girl, and saw every day that a brown, ingenuous Western witch was getting hobbles and a lasso on the young man you wanted for yourself, you, too, would lose taste for the oxidized-silver setting of a musical comedy.

Barbara sat by the quartered-oak library table. Her right arm rested upon the table, and her dextral fingers nervously manipulated a sealed letter. The letter was addressed to Nevada Warren; and in the upper left-hand corner of the envelope was Gilbert's little gold palette.
It had been delivered at nine o'clock, after Nevada had left.

Barbara would have given her pearl necklace to know what the letter contained; but she could not open and read it by the aid of steam, or a pen-handle, or a hair-pin, or any of the generally approved methods, because her position in society forbade such an act. She had tried to read some of the lines of the letter by holding the envelope up to a strong light and pressing it hard against the paper, but Gilbert had too good a taste in stationery to make that possible.

At eleven-thirty the theatre-goers returned. it was a delicious winter night. Even so far as from the cab to the door they were powdered thickly with the big flakes downpouring diagonally from the cast. Old Jerome growled good-naturedly about villanous cab service and blockaded streets. Nevada, colored like a rose, with sapphire eyes, babbled of the stormy nights in the mountains around dad's cabin. During all these wintry apostrophes, Barbara, cold at heart, sawed wood, the only appropriate thing she could think of to do.

Old Jerome went immediately up-stairs to hot-water-bottles and quinine. Nevada fluttered into the study, the only cheerfully lighted room, subsided into an arm-chair, and, while at the interminable task of unbuttoning her elbow gloves, gave oral testimony as to the demerits of the "show."

"Yes, I think Mr. Fields is really amusing sometimes," said Barbara. "Here is a letter for you, dear, that came by special delivery just after you had gone."

"Who is it from?" asked Nevada, tugging at a button.

"Well, really," said Barbara, with a smile, "I can only guess. The envelope has that queer little thing in one corner that Gilbert calls a palette, but which looks to me rather like a gilt heart on a school-girl's valentine."

"I wonder what he's writing to me about" remarked Nevada, listlessly.

"We're all alike," said Barbara; "all women. We try to find out what is in a letter by studying the postmark. As a last resort we use scissors, and read it from the bottom upward. Here it is."

She made a motion as if to toss the letter across the table to Nevada.

"Great catamounts!" exclaimed Nevada. "These centre-fire buttons are a nuisance. I'd rather wear buckskins. Oh, Barbara, please shuck the hide off that letter and read it. It'll be midnight before I get these gloves off!"

"Why, dear, you don't want me to open Gilbert's letter to you? It's for you, and you wouldn't wish anyone else to read it, of course!"

Nevada raised her steady, calm, sapphire eyes from her gloves.

"Nobody writes me anything that everybody mightn't read," she said. "Go on, Barbara. Maybe Gilbert wants us to go out in his car again to-morrow."

Curiosity can do more things than kill a cat; and if emotions, well recognized as feminine, are inimical to feline life, then jealousy would soon leave the whole world catless. Barbara opened the letter, with an indulgent, slightly bored air.

"Well, dear," said she, "I'll read it if you want me to."

She slit the envelope, and read the missive with swift-travelling eyes; read it again, and cast a quick, shrewd glance at Nevada, who, for the time, seemed to consider gloves as the world of her interest, and letters from rising artists as no more than messages from Mars.

For a quarter of a minute Barbara looked at Nevada with a strange steadfastness; and then a smile so small that it widened her mouth only the sixteenth part of an inch, and narrowed her eyes no more than a twentieth, flashed like an inspired thought across her face.

Since the beginning no woman has been a mystery to another woman Swift as light travels, each penetrates the heart and mind of another, sifts her sister's words of their cunningest disguises, reads her most hidden desires, and plucks the sophistry from her wiliest talk like hairs from a comb, twiddling them sardonically between her thumb and fingers before letting them float away on the breezes of fundamental doubt. Long ago Eve's son rang the door-bell of the family residence in Paradise Park, bearing a strange lady on his arm, whom he introduced. Eve took her daughter-in-law aside and lifted a classic eyebrow.

"The Land of Nod," said the bride, languidly flirting the leaf of a palm. "I suppose you've been there, of course?"

"Not lately," said Eve, absolutely unstaggered. "Don't you think the apple-sauce they serve over there is execrable? I rather like that mulberry-leaf tunic effect, dear; but, of course, the real fig goods are not to be had over there. Come over behind this lilac-bush while the gentlemen split a celery tonic. I think the caterpillar-holes have made your dress open a little in the back."

So, then and there, according to the records, was the alliance formed by the only two who's-who ladies in the world. Then it was agreed that woman should forever remain as clear as a pane of glass-though glass was yet to be discovered-to other women, and that she should palm herself off on man as a mystery.

Barbara seemed to hesitate.

"Really, Nevada," she said, with a little show of embarrassment, "you shouldn't have insisted on my opening this. I-I'm sure it wasn't meant for anyone else to know."

Nevada forgot her gloves for a moment.

"Then read it aloud," she said. "Since you've already read it, what's the difference? If Mr. Warren has written to me something that any one else oughtn't to know, that is all the more reason why everybody should know it."

"Well," said Barbara, "this is what it says:

'Dearest Nevada, Come to my studio at twelve o'clock to-night. Do not fail.'" Barbara rose and dropped the note in Nevada's lap. "I'm awfully sorry," she said, "that I knew. It isn't like Gilbert. There must be some mistake. Just consider that I am ignorant of it, will you, dear? I must go up-stairs now, I have such a headache. I'm sure I don't understand the note. Perhaps Gilbert has been dining too well, and will explain. Good night!"

IV
Nevada tiptoed to the hall, and heard Barbara's door close upstairs. The bronze clock in the study told the hour of twelve was fifteen minutes away. She ran swiftly to the front door, and let herself out into the snow-storm. Gilbert Warren's studio was six squares away.

By aerial ferry the white, silent forces of the storm attacked the city from beyond the sullen East River. Already the snow lay a foot deep on the pavements, the drifts heaping themselves like scaling-ladders against the walls of the besieged town. The Avenue was as quiet as a street in Pompeii. Cabs now and then skimmed past like white-winged gulls over a moonlit ocean; and less frequent motor-cars - sustaining the comparison, hissed through the foaming waves like submarine boats on their jocund, perilous journeys.

Nevada plunged like a wind-driven storm-petrel on her way. She looked up at the ragged sierras of cloud-capped buildings that rose above the streets, shaded by the night lights and the congealed vapors to gray, drab, ashen, lavender, dun, and cerulean tints. They were so like the wintry mountains of her Western home that she felt a satisfaction such as the hundred-thousand-dollar house had seldom brought her.

A policeman caused her to waver on a corner, just by his eye and weight.

"Hello, Mabel!" said he. "Kind of late for you to be out, ain't it?"

"I - I am just going to the drug store," said Nevada, hurrying past him.

The excuse serves as a passport for the most sophisticated. Does it prove that woman never progresses, or that she sprang from Adam's rib, full-fledged in intellect and wiles?

Turning eastward, the direct blast cut down Nevada's speed one-half.

She made zigzag tracks in the snow; but she was as tough as a pinon sapling, and bowed to it as gracefully. Suddenly the studio-building loomed before her, a familiar landmark, like a cliff above some well-remembered canon. The haunt of business and its hostile neighbor, art, was darkened and silent. The elevator stopped at ten.

Up eight flights of Stygian stairs Nevada climbed, and rapped firmly at the door numbered "89." She had been there many times before, with Barbara and Uncle Jerome.

Gilbert opened the door. He had a crayon pencil in one hand, a green shade over his eyes, and a pipe in his mouth. The pipe dropped to the floor.

"Am I late?" asked Nevada. "I came as quick as I could. Uncle and me were at the theatre this evening. Here I am, Gilbert!"

Gilbert did a Pygmalion-and-Galatea act. He changed from a statue of stupefaction to a young man with a problem to tackle. He admitted Nevada, got a whiskbroom, and began to brush the snow from her clothes. A great lamp, with a green shade, hung over an easel, where the artist had been sketching in crayon.

"You wanted me," said Nevada simply, "and I came. You said so in your letter. What did you send for me for?"

"You read my letter?" inquired Gilbert, sparring for wind.

"Barbara read it to me. I saw it afterward. It said: 'Come to my studio at twelve to-night, and do not fail.' I thought you were sick, of course, but you don't seem to be."

"Aha!" said Gilbert irrelevantly. "I'll tell you why I asked you to come, Nevada. I want you to marry me immediately - to-night. What's a little snow-storm? Will you do it?"

"You might have noticed that I would, long ago," said Nevada. "And I'm rather stuck on the snow-storm idea, myself. I surely would hate one of these flowery church noon-weddings. Gilbert, I didn't know you had grit enough to propose it this way. Let's shock 'em, it's our funeral, ain't it?"

"You bet!" said Gilbert. "Where did I hear that expression?" he added to himself. "Wait a minute, Nevada; I want to do a little 'phoning."

He shut himself in a little dressing-room, and called upon the lightnings of tile, heavens condensed into unromantic numbers and districts.

"That you, Jack? You confounded sleepyhead! Yes, wake up; this is
Me - or I - oh, bother the difference in grammar! I'm going to be
married right away. Yes! Wake up your sister, don't answer me back;
bring her along, too - you must!. Remind Agnes of the time I saved her
from drowning in Lake Ronkonkoma, I know it's caddish to refer to it,
but she must come with you. Yes. Nevada is here, waiting. We've
been engaged quite a while. Some opposition among the relatives, you
know, and we have to pull it off this way. We're waiting here for
you. Don't let Agnes out-talk you bring her! You will? Good old
boy! I'll order a carriage to call for you, double-quick time. Confound
you, Jack, you're all right!"

Gilbert returned to the room where Nevada waited.

"My old friend, Jack Peyton, and his sister were to have been here at
a quarter to twelve," he explained; "but Jack is so confoundedly slow.
I've just 'phoned them to hurry. They'll be here in a few minutes.
I'm the happiest man in the world, Nevada! What did you do with the
letter I sent you to-day ?"

"I've got it cinched here," said Nevada, pulling it out from beneath
her opera-cloak.

Gilbert drew the letter from the envelope and looked it over carefully.
Then he looked at Nevada thoughtfully.

"Didn't you think it rather queer that I should ask you to come to my
studio at midnight?" he asked.

"Why, no," said Nevada, rounding her eyes. "Not if you needed me.
Out West, when a pal sends you a hurry call, ain't that what you say
here? we get there first and talk about it after the row is over. And it's
usually snowing there, too, when things happen. So I didn't mind."

Gilbert rushed into another room, and came back burdened with
overcoats warranted to turn wind, rain, or snow.

"Put this raincoat on," he said, holding it for her. "We have a
quarter of a mile to go. Old Jack and his sister will be here in a
few minutes." He began to struggle into a heavy coat. "Oh, Nevada,"
he said, "just look at the head-lines on the front page of that
evening paper on the table, will you? It's about your section of the
West, and I know it will interest you."

He waited a full minute, pretending to find trouble in the getting on of his overcoat, and then turned. Nevada had not moved. She was looking at him with strange and pensive directness. Her cheeks had a flush on them beyond the color that had been contributed by the wind and snow; but her eyes were steady.

"I was going to tell you," she said, "anyhow, before you - before we- Before - well, before anything. Dad never gave me a day of schooling. I never learned to read or write a darned word. Now if -"

Pounding their uncertain way up-stairs, the feet of Jack, the somnolent, and Agnes, the grateful, were heard.

V

When Mr. and Mrs. Gilbert Warren were spinning softly homeward in a closed carriage, after the ceremony, Gilbert s said:

"Nevada, would you really like to know what I wrote you in the letter that you received to-night?"

"Fire away!" said his bride.

"Word for word," said Gilbert, "it was this: 'My dear Miss Warren-You were right about the flower. It was a hydrangea, and not a lilac.'

"All right," said Nevada. "But let's forget it. The joke's on Barbara, anyway!"

THIMBLE, THIMBLE

These are the directions for finding the I office of Carteret & Carteret, Mill Supplies and Leather Belting:

You follow the Broadway trail down until you pass the Crosstown Line, the Bread Line, and the Dead Line, and come to the Big Canons of the Moneygrubber Tribe. Then you turn to the left, to the right, dodge a push-cart and the tongue of a two-ton, four-horse dray and hop, skip, and jump to a granite ledge on the side of a twenty-one-story synthetic mountain of stone and iron. In the twelfth story is the office of Carteret & Carteret. The factory where they make the mill supplies and leather belting is in Brooklyn. Those commodities, to say nothing of Brooklyn, not being of interest to you, let us hold the incidents within the confines of a one-act, one-scene play, thereby lessening the toil of the reader and the expenditure of the publisher. So, if you have the courage to face four pages of type and Carteret & Carteret's office boy, Percival, you shall sit on a varnished chair in the inner office and peep at the little comedy of the Old Nigger Man, the Hunting-Case Watch, and the Open-Faced Question, mostly borrowed from the late Mr. Frank Stockton, as you will conclude.

First, biography (but pared to the quick) must intervene. I am for the inverted sugar-coated quinine pill - the bitter on the outside.

The Carterets were, or was (Columbia College professors please rule), an old Virginia family. Long time ago the gentlemen of the family had worn lace ruffles and carried tinless foils and owned plantations and had slaves to burn. But the war had greatly reduced their holdings. (Of course you can perceive at once that this flavor has been shoplifted from Mr. F. Hopkinson Smith, in spite of the "et" after "Carter.") Well, anyhow:

In digging up the Carteret history I shall not take you farther back than the year 1620. The two original American Carterets came over in that year, but by different means of transportation. One brother, named John, came in the Mayflower and became a Pilgrim Father. You've seen his picture on the covers of the Thanksgiving magazines, hunting turkeys in the deep snow with a blunderbuss. Blandford Carteret, the other brother, crossed the pond in his own brigantine, landed on the Virginia coast, and became an F.F.V. John became distinguished for piety and shrewdness in business; Blandford for his pride, juleps; marksmanship, and vast slave-cultivated plantations.

Then came the Civil War. (I must condense this historical interpolation.) Stonewall Jackson was shot; Lee surrendered; Grant

toured the world; cotton went to nine cents; Old Crow whiskey and Jim Crow cars were invented; the Seventy-ninth Massachusetts Volunteers returned to the Ninety-seventh Alabama Zouaves the battle flag of Lundy's Lane which they bought at a second-hand store in Chelsea kept by a man named Skzchnzski; Georgia sent the President a sixty-pound watermelon and that brings us up to the time when the story begins. My! but that was sparring for an opening! I really must brush op on my Aristotle.

The Yankee Carterets went into business in New York long before the war. Their house, as far as Leather Belting and Mill Supplies was concerned, was as musty and arrogant and solid as one of those old East India tea-importing concerns that you read about in Dickens. There were some rumors of a war behind its counters, but not enough to affect the business.

During and after the war, Blandford Carteret, F.F.V., lost his plantations, juleps, marksmanship, and life. He bequeathed little more than his pride to his surviving family. So it came to pass that Blandford Carteret, the Fifth, aged fifteen, was invited by the leather-and-millsupplies branch of that name to come North and learn business instead of hunting foxes and boasting of the glory of his fathers on the reduced acres of his impoverished family. The boy jumped at the chance; and, at the age of twenty-five, sat in the office of the firm equal partner with John, the Fifth, of the blunderbuss-and-turkey branch. Here the story begins again.

The young men were about the same age, smooth of face, alert, easy of manner, and with an air that promised mental and physical quickness. They were razored, blue-serged, straw-hatted, and pearl stick-pinned like other young New Yorkers who might be millionaires or bill clerks.

One afternoon at four o'clock, in the private office of the firm, Blandford Carteret opened a letter that a clerk had just brought to his desk. After reading it, he chuckled audibly for nearly a minute. John looked around from his desk inquiringly.

"It's from mother," said Blandford. "I'll read you the funny part of it. She tells me all the neighborhood news first, of course, and then cautions me against getting my feet wet and musical comedies. After that come some vital statistics about calves and pigs and an estimate of the wheat crop. And now I'll quote some:

"'And what do you think! Old Uncle Jake, who was seventy-six last Wednesday, must go travelling. Nothing would do but he must go to New York and see his "young Marster Blandford." Old as he is, he has a deal of common sense, so I've let him go. I couldn't refuse him, he seemed to have concentrated all his hopes and desires into this one adventure into the wide world. You know he was born on the plantation, and has never been ten miles away from it in his life. And he was your father's body servant during the war, and has been always a faithful vassal and servant of the family. He has often seen the gold watch, the watch that was your father's and your father's father's. I told him it was to be yours, And he begged me to allow him to take it to you and to put it into your hands himself.

"'So he has it, carefully inclosed in a buck-skin case, and is bringing it to you with all the pride and importance of a king's messenger. I gave him money for the round trip and for a two weeks' stay in the city. I wish you would see to it that he gets comfortable quarters, Jake won't need much looking after, he's able to take care of himself. But I have read in the papers that African bishops and colored potentates generally have much trouble in obtaining food and lodging in the Yankee metropolis. That may be all right; but I don't see why the best hotel there shouldn't take Jake in. Still, I suppose it's a rule.

"'I gave him full directions about finding you, and packed his valise myself. You won't have to bother with him; but I do hope you'll see that he is made comfortable. Take the watch that he brings you, it's almost a decoration. It has been worn by true Carterets, and there isn't a stain upon it nor a false movement of the wheels. Bringing it to you is the crowning joy of old Jake's life. I wanted him to have that little outing and that happiness before it is too late. You have often heard us talk about how Jake, pretty badly wounded himself, crawled through the reddened grass at Chancellorsville to where your father lay with the bullet in his dear heart, and took the watch from his pocket to keep it from the "Yanks."

"'So, my son, when the old man comes consider him as a frail but worthy messenger from the old-time life and home.

"'You have been so long away from home and so long among the people that we have always regarded as aliens that I'm not sure that Jake will know you when he sees you. But Jake has a keen perception, and I rather believe that he will know a Virginia Carteret at sight. I can't conceive that even ten years in Yankee-land could change a boy of mine. Anyhow, I'm sure you will know Jake. I put eighteen collars in his valise. If he should have to buy others, he wears a number 15 1/2. Please see that he gets the right ones. He will be no trouble to you at all.

"'If you are not too busy, I'd like for you to find him a place to board where they have white-meal corn-bread, and try to keep him from taking his shoes off in your office or on the street. His right foot swells a little, and he likes to be comfortable.

"'If you can spare the time, count his handkerchiefs when they come back from the wash. I bought him a dozen new ones before he left. He should be there about the time this letter reaches you. I told him to go straight to your office when he arrives.'"

As soon as Blandford had finished the reading of this, something happened (as there should happen in stories and must happen on the stage).

Percival, the office boy, with his air of despising the world's output of mill supplies and leather belting, came in to announce that a colored gentleman was outside to see Mr. Blandford Carteret.

"Bring him in," said Blandford, rising.

John Carteret swung around in his chair and said to Percival: "Ask him to wait a few minutes outside. We'll let you know when to bring him in."

Then he turned to his cousin with one of those broad, slow smiles that was an inheritance of all the Carterets, and said:

"Bland, I've always had a consuming curiosity to understand the differences that you haughty Southerners believe to exist between 'you all ' and the people of the North. Of course, I know that you consider yourselves made out of finer clay and look upon Adam as only a collateral branch of your ancestry; but I don't know why. I never could understand the differences between us."

"Well, John," said Blandford, laughing, "what you don't understand about it is just the difference, of course. I suppose it was the feudal way in which we lived that gave us our lordly baronial airs and feeling of superiority."

"But you are not feudal, now," went on John. "Since we licked you and stole your cotton and mules you've had to go to work just as we 'damyankees,' as you call us, have always been doing. And you're just as proud and exclusive and upper-classy as you were before the war. So it wasn't your money that caused it."

"Maybe it was the climate," said Blandford, lightly, "or maybe our negroes spoiled us. I'll call old Jake in, now. I'll be glad to see the old villain again."

"Wait just a moment," said John. "I've got a little theory I want to test. You and I are pretty much alike in our general appearance. Old Jake hasn't seen you since you were fifteen. Let's have him in and play fair and see which of us gets the watch. The old darky surrey ought to be able to pick out his 'young marster' without any trouble. The alleged aristocratic superiority of a 'reb' ought to be visible to him at once. He couldn't make the mistake of handing over the timepiece to a Yankee, of course. The loser buys the dinner this evening and two dozen 15 1/2 collars for Jake. Is it a go?"

Blandford agreed heartily. Percival was summoned, and told to usher the "colored gentleman" in.

Uncle Jake stepped inside the private office cautiously. He was a little old man, as black as soot, wrinkled and bald except for a fringe of white wool, cut decorously short, that ran over his ears and around his head. There was nothing of the stage "uncle" about him: his black suit nearly fitted him; his shoes shone, and his straw hat was banded with a gaudy ribbon. In his right hand he carried something carefully concealed by his closed fingers.

Uncle Jake stopped a few steps from the door. Two young men sat in their revolving desk-chairs ten feet apart and looked at him in friendly silence. His gaze slowly shifted many times from one to the other. He felt sure that he was in the presence of one, at least, of the revered family among whose fortunes his life had begun and was to end.

One had the pleasing but haughty Carteret air; the other had the unmistakable straight, long family nose. Both had the keen black eyes, horizontal brows, and thin, smiling lips that had distinguished both the Carteret of the Mayflower and him of the brigantine. Old Jake had thought that he could have picked out his young master instantly from a thousand Northerners; but he found himself in difficulties. The best he could do was to use strategy.

"Howdy, Marse Blandford, howdy, suh ?" he said, looking midway between the two young men.

"Howdy, Uncle Jake?" they both answered pleasantly and in unison. "Sit down. Have you brought the watch?"

Uncle Jake chose a hard-bottom chair at a respectful distance, sat on the edge of it, and laid his hat carefully on the floor. The watch in its buckskin case he gripped tightly. He had not risked his life on the battle-field to rescue that watch from his "old marster's" foes to hand it over again to the enemy without a struggle.

"Yes, suh; I got it in my hand, suh. I'm gwine give it to you right away in jus' a minute. Old Missus told me to put it in young Marse Blandford's hand and tell him to wear it for the family pride and honor. It was a mighty longsome trip for an old nigger man to make, ten thousand miles, it must be, back to old Vi'ginia, suh. You've growed mightily, young marster. I wouldn't have reconnized you but for yo' powerful resemblance to old marster."

With admirable diplomacy the old man kept his eyes roaming in the space between the two men. His words might have been addressed to either. Though neither wicked nor perverse, he was seeking for a sign.

Blandford and John exchanged winks.

"I reckon you done got you ma's letter," went on Uncle Jake. "She said she was gwine to write to you 'bout my comin' along up this er-way.

"Yes, yes, Uncle Jake," said John briskly. "My cousin and I have just been notified to expect you. We are both Carterets, you know."

"Although one of us," said Blandford, "was born and raised in the North."

"So if you will hand over the watch -" said John.

"My cousin and I-" said Blandford.

'Will then see to it -" said John.

"That comfortable quarters are found for you," said Blandford.

With creditable ingenuity, old Jake set up a cackling, high-pitched, protracted laugh. He beat his knee, picked up his hat and bent the brim in an apparent paroxysm of humorous appreciation. The seizure afforded him a mask behind which he could roll his eyes impartially between, above, and beyond his two tormentors.

"I sees what!" he chuckled, after a while. "You gen'lemen is tryin' to have fun with the po' old nigger. But you can't fool old Jake. I knowed you, Marse Blandford, the minute I sot eyes on you. You was a po' skimpy little boy no mo' than about fo'teen when you lef' home to come No'th; but I knowed you the minute I sot eyes on you. You is the mawtal image of old marster. The other gen'leman resembles you mightily, suh; but you can't fool old Jake on a member of the old Vi'ginia family. No suh."

At exactly the same time both Carterets smiled and extended a hand for the watch.

Uncle Jake's wrinkled, black face lost the expression of amusement to which he had vainly twisted it. He knew that he was being teased, and that it made little real difference, as far as its safety went, into which of those outstretched hands he placed the family treasure. But it seemed to him that not only his own pride and loyalty but much of the Virginia Carterets' was at stake. He had heard down South during the war about that other branch of the family that lived in the North and fought on "the yuther side," and it had always grieved him. He had followed his "old marster's" fortunes from stately luxury through war to almost poverty. And now, with the last relic and reminder of him, blessed by "old missus," and intrusted implicitly to his care, he had come ten thousand miles (as it seemed) to deliver it into the hands of the one who was to wear it and wind it and cherish it and listen to it tick off the unsullied hours that marked the lives of the Carterets, of Virginia.

His experience and conception of the Yankees had been an impression of Tyrants "low-down, common trash" in blue, laying waste with fire and sword. He had seen the smoke of many burning homesteads almost as grand as Carteret Hall ascending to the drowsy Southern skies. And now he was face to face with one of them and he could not distinguish him from his "young marster" whom he had come to find and bestow upon him the emblem of his kingship, even as the arm "clothed in white samite, mystic, wonderful" laid Excalibur in the right hand of Arthur. He saw before him two young men, easy, kind, courteous, welcoming, either of whom might have been the one he sought. Troubled, bewildered, sorely grieved at his weakness of judgment, old Jake abandoned his loyal subterfuges. His right hand sweated against the buckskin cover of the watch. He was deeply humiliated and chastened. Seriously, now, his prominent, yellow-white eyes closely scanned the two young men. At the end of his scrutiny he was conscious of but one difference between them. One wore a narrow black tie with a white pearl stickpin. The other's "four-in-hand " was a narrow blue one pinned with a black pearl.

And then, to old Jake's relief, there came a sudden distraction. Drama knocked at the door with imperious knuckles, and forced Comedy to the wings, and Drama peeped with a smiling but set face over the footlights.

Percival, the hater of mill supplies, brought in a card, which he handed, with the manner of one bearing a cartel, to Blue-Tie.

"'Olivia De Ormond,'" read Blue-Tie from the card. He looked inquiringly at his cousin.

"Why not have her in," said Black-Tie, "and bring matters to a conclusion?"

"Uncle Jake," said one of the young men, "would you mind taking that chair over there in the corner for a while? A lady is coming in on some business. We'll take up your case afterward."

The lady whom Percival ushered in was young and petulantly, decidedly, freshly, consciously, and intentionally pretty. She was dressed with such expensive plainness that she made you consider lace and ruffles as mere tatters and rags. But one great ostrich plume that she wore would have marked her anywhere in the army of beauty as the wearer of the merry helmet of Navarre.

Miss De Ormond accepted the swivel chair at Blue-Tie's desk. Then the gentlemen drew leather-upholstered seats conveniently near, and spoke of the weather.

"Yes," said she, "I noticed it was warmer. But I mustn't take up too much of your time during business hours. That is," she continued, "unless we talk business."

She addressed her words to Blue-Tie, with a charming smile.

"Very well," said he. "You don't mind my cousin being present, do you? We are generally rather confidential with each other-especially in business matters."

"Oh no," caroled Miss De Ormond. "I'd rather he did hear. He knows all about it, anyhow. In fact, he's quite a material witness because he was present when you - when it happened. I thought you might want to talk things over before well, before any action is taken, as I believe the lawyers say."

"Have you anything in the way of a proposition to make?" asked Black-Tie.

Miss De Ormond looked reflectively at the neat toe of one of her dull kid-pumps.

"I had a proposal made to me," she said. "If the proposal sticks it cuts out the proposition. Let's have that settled first."

"Well, as far as -" began Blue-Tie.

"Excuse me, cousin," interrupted Black-Tie, "if you don't mind my cutting in." And then he turned, with a good-natured air, toward the lady.

"Now, let's recapitulate a bit," he said cheerfully. "All three of us, besides other mutual acquaintances, have been out on a good many larks together."

"I'm afraid I'll have to call the birds by another name," said Miss De Ormond.

"All right," responded Black-Tie, with unimpaired cheerfulness; "suppose we say 'squabs' when we talk about the 'proposal' and 'larks' when we discuss the 'proposition.' You have a quick mind, Miss De Ormond. Two months ago some half-dozen of us went in a motor-car for day's run into the country. We stopped at a road-house for dinner. My cousin proposed marriage to you then and there. He was influenced to do so, of course, by the beauty and charm which no one can deny that you possess."

"I wish I had you for a press agent, Mr. Carteret," said the beauty, with a dazzling smile.

"You are on the stage, Miss De Ormond," went on Black-Tie. "You have had, doubtless, many admirers, and perhaps other proposals. You must remember, too, that we were a party of merrymakers on that occasion. There were a good many corks pulled. That the proposal of marriage was made to you by my cousin we cannot deny. But hasn't it been your experience that, by common consent, such things lose their seriousness when viewed in the next day's sunlight? Isn't there something of a 'code' among good 'sports' I use the word in its best sense, that wipes out each day the follies of the evening previous?"

"Oh yes," said Miss De Ormond. "I know that very well. And I've always played up to it. But as you seem to be conducting the case with the silent consent of the defendant I'll tell you something more. I've got letters from him repeating the proposal. And they're signed, too."

"I understand," said Black-Tie gravely. "What's your price for the letters?"

"I'm not a cheap one," said Miss De Ormond. "But I had decided to make you a rate. You both belong to a swell family. Well, if I am on the stage nobody can say a word against me truthfully. And the money is only a secondary consideration. It isn't the money I was after. I - I believed him - and - and I liked him."

She cast a soft, entrancing glance at Blue-Tie from under her long eyelashes.

"And the price?" went on Black-Tie, inexorably.

"Ten thousand dollars," said the lady, sweetly.

"Or -"

"Or the fulfillment of the engagement to marry."

"I think it is time," interrupted Blue-Tie, "for me to be allowed to say a word or two. You and I, cousin, belong to a family that has held its head pretty high. You have been brought up in a section of the country very different from the one where our branch of the family lived. Yet both of us are Carterets, even if some of our ways and theories differ. You remember, it is a tradition of the family, that no Carteret ever failed in chivalry to a lady or failed to keep his word when it was given."

Then Blue-Tie, with frank decision showing on his countenance, turned to Miss De Ormond.

"Olivia," said he, "on what date will you marry me?"

Before she could answer, Black-Tie again interposed.

"It is a long journey," said he, "from Plymouth rock to Norfolk Bay. Between the two points we find the changes that nearly three centuries have brought. In that time the old order has changed. We no longer burn witches or torture slaves. And to-day we neither spread our cloaks on the mud for ladies to walk over nor treat them to the ducking-stool. It is the age of common sense, adjustment, and proportion. All of us, ladies, gentlemen, women, men, Northerners, Southerners, lords, caitiffs, actors, hardware-drummers, senators, hodcarriers, and politicians are coming to a better understanding. Chivalry is one of our words that changes its meaning every day. Family pride is a thing of many constructions - it may show itself by maintaining a moth-eaten arrogance in cobwebbed Colonial mansion or by the prompt paying of one's debts.

"Now, I suppose you've had enough of my monologue. I've learned something of business and a little of life; and I somehow believe, cousin, that our great-great-grandfathers, the original Carterets, would indorse my view of this matter."

Black-Tie wheeled around to his desk, wrote in a check-book and tore out the check, the sharp rasp of the perforated leaf making the only sound in the room. He laid the check within easy reach of Miss De Ormond's hand.

"Business is business," said he. "We live in a business age. There is my personal check for $10,000. What do you say, Miss De Ormond, will it he orange blossoms or cash ?"

Miss De Ormond picked up the cheek carelessly, folded it indifferently, and stuffed it into her glove.

"Oh, this '11 do," she said, calmly. "I just thought I'd call and put it up to you. I guess you people are all right. But a girl has feelings, you know. I've heard one of you was a Southerner, I wonder which one of you it is?"

She arose, smiled sweetly, and walked to the door. There, with a flash of white teeth and a dip of the heavy plume, she disappeared.

Both of the cousins had forgotten Uncle Jake for the time. But now they heard the shuffling of his shoes as he came across the rug toward them from his seat in the corner.

"Young marster," he said, "take yo' watch." And without hesitation he laid the ancient timepiece in the hand of its rightful owner.

Finch keeps a hats-cleaned-by-electricity-while-you-wait establishment, nine feet by twelve, in Third Avenue. Once a customer, you are always his. I do not know his secret process, but every four days your hat needs to be cleaned again.

Finch is a leathern, sallow, slowfooted man, between twenty and forty. You would say he had been brought up a bushelman in Essex Street. When business is slack he likes to talk, so I had my hat cleaned even oftener than it deserved, hoping Finch might let me into some of the secrets of the sweatshops.

One afternoon I dropped in and found Finch alone. He began to anoint my headpiece de Panama with his mysterious fluid that attracted dust and dirt like a magnet.

"They say the Indians weave 'em under water," said I, for a leader.

"Don't you believe it," said Finch. "No Indian or white man could stay under water that long. Say, do you pay much attention to politics? I see in the paper something about a law they've passed called 'the law of supply and demand.'"

I explained to him as well as I could that the reference was to a politico-economical law, and not to a legal statute.

"I didn't know," said Finch. "I heard a good deal about it a year or so ago, but in a one-sided way."

"Yes," said I, "political orators use it a great deal. In fact, they never give it a rest. I suppose you heard some of those cart-tail fellows spouting on the subject over here on the east side."

"I heard it from a king," said Finch "the white king of a tribe of Indians in South America."

I was interested but not surprised. The big city is like a mother's knee to many who have strayed far and found the roads rough beneath their uncertain feet. At dusk they come home and sit upon the doorstep. I know a piano player in a cheap cafe who has shot lions in Africa, a bell-boy who fought in the British army against the Zulus, an express-driver whose left arm had been cracked like a lobster's claw for a stew-pot of Patagonian cannibals when the boat of his rescuers hove in sight. So a hat-cleaner who had been a friend of a king did not oppress me.

"A new band ?" asked Finch, with his dry, barren smile.

"Yes," said I, "and half an inch wider." I had had a new band five days before.

"I meets a man one night," said Finch, beginning his story "a man brown as snuff, with money in every pocket, eating schweinerknuckel in Schlagel's. That was two years ago, when I was a hose-cart driver for No. 98. His discourse runs to the subject of gold. He says that certain mountains in a country down South that he calls Gaudymala is full of it. He says the Indians wash it out of the streams in plural quantities.

"'Oh, Geronimo!' says I. 'Indians! There's no Indians in the South,' I tell him, 'except Elks, Maccabees, and the buyers for the fall dry-goods trade. The Indians are all on the reservations,' says I.

"'I'm telling you this with reservations,' says he. 'They ain't Buffalo Bill Indians; they're squattier and more pedigreed. They call 'em Inkers and Aspics, and they was old inhabitants when Mazuma was King of Mexico. They wash the gold out of the mountain streams,' says the brown man, 'and fill quills with it; and then they empty 'em into red jars till they are full; and then they pack it in buckskin sacks of one arroba each, an arroba is twenty-five pounds and store it in a stone house, with an engraving of a idol with marcelled hair, playing a flute, over the door.'

"'how do they work off this unearth increment?' I asks.

"'They don't,' says the man. 'It's a case of "Ill fares the land with the great deal of velocity where wealth accumulates and there ain't any reciprocity."'

"After this man and me got through our conversation, which left him dry of information, I shook hands with him and told him I was sorry I couldn't believe him. And a month afterward I landed on the coast of this Gaudymala with $1,300 that I had been saving up for five years. I thought I knew what Indians liked, and I fixed myself accordingly. I loaded down four pack-mules with red woollen blankets, wrought-iron pails, jewelled side-combs for the ladies, glass necklaces, and safety-razors. I hired a black mozo, who was supposed to be a mule-driver and an interpreter too. It turned out that he could interpret mules all right, but he drove the English language much too hard. His name sounded like a Yale key when you push it in wrong side up, but I called him McClintock, which was close to the noise.

"Well, this gold village was forty miles up in the mountains, and it took us nine days to find it. But one afternoon McClintock led the other mules and myself over a rawhide bridge stretched across a precipice five thousand feet deep, it seemed to me. The hoofs of the beasts drummed on it just like before George M. Cohan makes his first entrance on the stage.

"This village was built of mud and stone, and had no streets. Some few yellow-and-brown persons popped their heads out-of-doors, looking about like Welsh rabbits with Worcester sauce on em. Out of the biggest house, that had a kind of a porch around it, steps a big white man, red as a beet in color, dressed in fine tanned deerskin clothes, with a gold chain around his neck, smoking a cigar. I've seen United States Senators of his style of features and build, also head-waiters and cops.

"He walks up and takes a look at us, while McClintock disembarks and begins to interpret to the lead mule while he smokes a cigarette.

"'Hello, Buttinsky,' says the fine man to me. 'How did you get in the game? I didn't see you buy any chips. Who gave you the keys of the city?'

"'I'm a poor traveller,' says I. 'Especially mule-back. You'll excuse me. Do you run a hack line or only a bluff?'

"'Segregate yourself from your pseudo-equine quadruped,' says he, 'and come inside.'

"He raises a finger, and a villager runs up.

"'This man will take care of your outfit,' says he, 'and I'll take care of you.'

"He leads me into the biggest house, and sets out the chairs and a kind of a drink the color of milk. It was the finest room I ever saw. The stone walls was hung all over with silk shawls, and there was red and yellow rugs on the floor, and jars of red pottery and Angora goat skins, and enough bamboo furniture to misfurnish half a dozen seaside cottages.

"'In the first place,' says the man, 'you want to know who I am. I'm sole lessee and proprietor of this tribe of Indians. They call me the Grand Yacuma, which is to say King or Main Finger of the bunch. I've got more power here than a charge d'affaires, a charge of dynamite, and a charge account at Tiffany's combined. In fact, I'm the Big Stick, with as many extra knots on it as there is on the record run of the Lusitania. Oh, I read the papers now and then,' says he. 'Now, let's hear your entitlements,' he goes on, 'and the meeting will be open.'

"'Well,' says I, 'I am known as one W. D. Finch. Occupation, capitalist. Address, 54' East Thirty-second -'

"'New York,' chips in the Noble Grand. 'I know,' says he, grinning. 'It ain't the first time you've seen it go down on the blotter. I can tell by the way you hand it out. Well, explain "capitalist."'

"I tells this boss plain what I come for and how I come to came.

"'Gold-dust?' says he, looking as puzzled as a baby that's got a feather stuck on its molasses finger. 'That's funny. This ain't a gold-mining country. And you invested all your capital on a stranger's story? Well, well! These Indians of mine, they are the last of the tribe of Peehes, are simple as children. They know nothing of the purchasing power of gold. I'm afraid you've been imposed on,' says he.

"'Maybe so,' says I, 'but it sounded pretty straight to me.'

"'W. D.,' says the King, all of a sudden, 'I'll give you a square deal. It ain't often I get to talk to a white man, and I'll give you a show for your money. It may be these constituents of mine have a few grains of gold-dust hid away in their clothes. To-morrow you may get out these goods you've brought up and see if you can make any sales. Now, I'm going to introduce myself unofficially. My name is Shane, Patrick Shane. I own this tribe of Peche Indians by right of Conquest, single handed and unafraid. I drifted up here four years ago, and won 'em by my size and complexion and nerve. I learned their language in six weeks-it's easy: you simply emit a string of consonants as long as your breath holds out and then point at what you're asking for.

"'I conquered 'em, spectacularly,' goes on King Shane, 'and then I went at 'em with economical politics, law, sleight-of-hand, and a kind of New England ethics and parsimony. Every Sunday, or as near as I can guess at it, I preach to 'em in the council-house (I'm the council) on the law of supply and demand. I praise supply and knock demand. I use the same text every time. You wouldn't think, W. D.,' says Shane, 'that I had poetry in me, would you?'

"'Well,' says I, 'I wouldn't know whether to call it poetry or not.'

"'Tennyson,' says Shane, 'furnishes the poetic gospel I preach. I always considered him the boss poet. Here's the way the text goes:

"For, not to admire, if a man could learn it, were more
Than to walk all day like a Sultan of old in a garden of spice."

"'You see, I teach 'em to cut out demand, that supply is the main thing. I teach 'em not to desire anything beyond their simplest needs. A little mutton, a little cocoa, and a little fruit brought up from the coast, that's all they want to make 'cm happy. I've got 'em well trained. They make their own clothes and hats out of a vegetable fibre and straw, and they're a contented lot. It's a great thing,' winds up Shane, 'to have made a people happy by the incultivation of such simple institutions.'

"Well, the next day, with the King's permission, I has the McClintock open up a couple of sacks of my goods in the little plaza of the village. The Indians swarmed around by the hundred and looked the bargain-counter over. I shook red blankets at 'em, flashed finger-rings and ear-bobs, tried pearl necklaces and sidecombs on the women, and a line of red hosiery on the men. 'Twas no use. They looked on like hungry graven images, but I never made a sale. I asked McClintock what was the trouble. Mac yawned three or four times, rolled a cigarette, made one or two confidential side remarks to a mule, and then condescended to inform me that the people had no money.

"Just then up strolls King Patrick, big and red 'and royal as usual, with the gold chain over his chest and his cigar in front of him.

"'How's business, W. D.?' he asks.

"'Fine,' says I. 'It's a bargain-day rush. I've got one more line of goods to offer before I shut up shop. I'll try 'em with safety-razors. I've' got two gross that I bought at 'a fire sale.'

"Shane laughs till some kind of mameluke or private secretary he carries with him has to hold him up.

"'0 my sainted Aunt Jerusha!' says he, 'ain't you one of the Babes in the Goods, W. D.? Don't you know that no Indians ever shave? They pull out their whiskers instead.'

"'Well,' says I, 'that's just what these razors would do for 'em, they wouldn't have any kick coming if they used 'em once.'

"Shane went away, and I could hear him laughing a block, if there had been any block.

"'Tell 'em,' says I to McClintock, 'it ain't money I want tell 'em I'll take gold-dust. Tell 'em I'll allow 'em sixteen dollars an ounce for it in trade. That's what I'm out for - the dust.'

"Mac interprets, and you'd have thought a squadron of cops had charged the crowd to disperse it. Every uncle's nephew and aunt's niece of 'em faded away inside of two minutes.

"At the royal palace that night me and the King talked it over.

"'They've got the dust hid out somewhere,' says I, 'or they wouldn't have been so sensitive about it.'

"'They haven't,' says Shane. 'What's this gag you've got about gold? You been reading Edward Allen Poe? They ain't got any gold.'

"'They put it in quills,' says I, 'and then they empty it in jars, and then into sacks of twenty-five pounds each. I got it straight.'

"'W. D.,' says Shane, laughing and chewing his cigar, 'I don't often see a white man, and I feel like putting you on. I don't think you'll get away from here alive, anyhow, so I'm going to tell you. Come over here.'

"He draws aside a silk fibre curtain in a corner of the room and shows me a pile of buckskin sacks.

"'Forty of 'em,' says Shane. 'One arroba in each one. In round numbers, $220,000 worth of gold-dust you see there. It's all mine. It belongs to the Grand Yacuma. They bring it all to me. Two hundred and twenty thousand dollars, think of that, you glass-bead peddler,' says Shane -' and all mine.'

"'Little good it does you,' says I, contemptuously and hatefully. 'And so you are the government depository of this gang of money-less money-makers? Don't you pay enough interest on it to enable one of your depositors to buy an Augusta (Maine) Pullman carbon diamond worth $200 for $4.85 ?'

"'Listen,' says Patrick Shane, with the sweat coming out on his brow.

' I'm confident with you, as you have, somehow, enlisted my regards. Did you ever,' he says, 'feel the avoirdupois power of gold, not the troy weight of it, but the sixteen-ounces-to-the-pound force of it?'

"'Never,' says I. 'I never take in any bad money.'

"Shane drops down on the floor and throws his arms over the sacks of gold-dust.

"'I love it,, says he. 'I want to feel the touch of it day and night. It's my pleasure in life. I come in this room, and I'm a king and a rich man. I'll be a millionaire in another year. The pile's getting bigger every month. I've got the whole tribe washing out the sands in the creeks. I'm the happiest man in the world, W. D. I just want to be near this gold, and know it's mine and it's increasing every day. Now, you know,' says he, 'why my Indians wouldn't buy your goods. They can't. They bring all the dust to me. I'm their king. I've taught 'em not to desire or admire. You might as well shut up shop.'

"'I'll tell you what you are,' says I. 'You're a plain, contemptible miser. You preach supply and you forget demand. Now, supply,' I goes on, 'is never anything but supply. On the contrary,' says I, 'demand is a much broader syllogism and assertion. Demand includes the rights of our women and children, and charity and friendship, and even a little begging on the street corners. They've both got to harmonize equally. And I've got a few things up my commercial sleeve yet,' says I, 'that may jostle your preconceived ideas of politics and economy.

"The next morning I had McClintock bring tip another mule-load of goods to the plaza and open it up. The people gathered around the same as before.

"I got out the finest line of necklaces, bracelets, hair-combs, and earrings that I carried, and had the women put 'em on. And then I played trumps.

"Out of my last pack I opened up a half gross of hand-mirrors, with solid tinfoil backs, and passed 'em around among the ladies. That was the first introduction of looking-glasses among the Peche Indians.

"Shane walks by with his big laugh.

"'Business looking up any?' he asks.

"'It's looking at itself right now,' says I.

"By-and-by a kind of a murmur goes through the crowd. The women had looked into the magic crystal and seen that they were beautiful, and was confiding the secret to the men. The men seemed to be urging the lack of money and the hard times just before the election, but their excuses didn't go.

"Then was my time.

"I called McClintock away from an animated conversation with his mules and told him to do some interpreting.

"'Tell 'em,' says I, 'that gold-dust will buy for them these befitting ornaments for kings and queens of the earth. Tell 'em the yellow sand they wash out of the waters for the High Sanctified Yacomay and Chop Suey of the tribe will buy the precious jewels and charms that will make them beautiful and preserve and pickle them from evil spirits. Tell 'em the Pittsburg banks are paying four per cent. interest on deposits by mail, while this get-rich-frequently custodian of the public funds ain't even paying attention. Keep telling 'em, Mac,' says I, 'to let the gold-dust family do their work. Talk to 'em like a born anti-Bryanite,' says I. 'Remind 'em that Tom Watson's gone back to Georgia,' says I.

"McClintock waves his hand affectionately at one of his mules, and then hurls a few stickfuls of minion type at the mob of shoppers.

"A gutta-percha Indian man, with a lady hanging on his arm, with three strings of my fish-scale jewelry and imitation marble beads around her neck, stands up on a block of stone and makes a talk that sounds like a man shaking dice in a box to fill aces and sixes.

"'He says,' says McClintock, 'that the people not know that gold-dust will buy their things. The women very mad. The Grand Yacuma tell them it no good but for keep to make bad spirits keep away.'

"'You can't keep bad spirits away from money,' says I.

"'They say,' goes on McClintock, 'the Yacuma fool them. They raise plenty row.'

"'Going! Going!' says I. 'Gold-dust or cash takes the entire stock. The dust weighed before you, and taken at sixteen dollars the ounce, the highest price on the Gaudymala coast.'

"Then the crowd disperses all of a sudden, and I don't know what's up. Mac and me packs away the hand-mirrors and jewelry they had handed back to us, and we had the mules back to the corral they had set apart for our garage.

"While we was there we hear great noises of shouting, and down across the plaza runs Patrick Shane, hotfoot, with his clothes ripped half off, and scratches on his face like a cat had fought him hard for every one of its lives.

"'They're looting the treasury, W. D.,' he sings out. 'They're going to kill me and you, too. Unlimber a couple of mules at once. We'll have to make a get-away in a couple of minutes.'

"'They've found out,' says I,' the truth about the law of supply and demand.'

"'It's the women, mostly,' says the King. 'And they used to admire me so!'

"'They hadn't seen looking-glasses then,' says I.

"'They've got knives and hatchets,' says Shane; 'hurry !'

"'Take that roan mule,' says I. 'You and your law of supply! I'll ride the dun, for he's two knots per hour the faster. The roan has a stiff knee, but he may make it,' says I. 'If you'd included reciprocity in your political platform I might have given you the dun,' says I.

"Shane and McClintock and me mounted our mules and rode across the rawhide bridge just as the Peches reached the other side and began firing stones and long knives at us. We cut the thongs that held up our end of the bridge and headed for the coast."

A tall, bulky policeman came into Finch's shop at that moment and leaned an elbow on the showcase. Finch nodded at him friendly.

"I heard down at Casey's," said the cop, in rumbling, husky tones, "that there was going to be a picnic of the Hat-Cleaners' Union over at Bergen Beach, Sunday. Is that right?"

"Sure," said Finch. "There'll be a dandy time."

"Gimme five tickets," said the cop, throwing a five-dollar bill on the showcase.

"Why," said Finch, "ain't you going it a little too -"

"Go to h -!" said the cop. "You got 'em to sell, ain't you? Somebody's got to buy 'em. Wish I could go along."

I was glad to See Finch so well thought of in his neighborhood.

And then in came a wee girl of seven, with dirty face and pure blue eyes and a smutched and insufficient dress.

"Mamma says," she recited shrilly, "that you must give me eighty cents for the grocer and nineteen for the milkman and five cents for me to buy hokey-pokey with but she didn't say that," the elf concluded, with a hopeful but honest grin.

Finch shelled out the money, counting it twice, but I noticed that the total sum that the small girl received was one dollar and four cents.

"That's the right kind of a law," remarked Finch, as he carefully broke some of the stitches of my hatband so that it would assuredly come off within a few days "the law of supply and demand. But they've both got to work together. I'll bet," he went on, with his dry smile, "she'll get jelly beans with that nickel, she likes 'em. What's supply if there's no demand for it?"

"Whatever became of the King?" I asked, curiously.

"Oh, I might have told you," said Finch. "That was Shane came in and bought the tickets. He came back with me, and he's on the force now."

BURIED TREASURE

There are many kinds of fools. Now, will everybody please sit still until they are called upon specifically to rise?

I had been every kind of fool except one. I had expended my patrimony, pretended my matrimony, played poker, lawn-tennis, and bucket-shops, parted soon with my money in many ways. But there remained one rule of the wearer of cap and bells that I had not played. That was the Seeker after Buried Treasure. To few does the delectable furor come. But of all the would-be followers in the hoof-prints of King Midas none has found a pursuit so rich in pleasurable promise.

But, going back from my theme a while, as lame pens must do, I was a fool of the sentimental soft. I saw May Martha Mangum, and was hers. She was eighteen, the color of the white ivory keys of a new piano, beautiful, and possessed by the exquisite solemnity and pathetic witchery of an unsophisticated angel doomed to live in a small, dull, Texas prairie-town. She had a spirit and charm that could have enabled her to pluck rubies like raspberries from the crown of Belgium or any other sporty kingdom, but she did not know it, and I did not paint the picture for her.

You see, I wanted May Martha Mangum for to have and to hold. I wanted her to abide with me, and put my slippers and pipe away every day in places where they cannot be found of evenings.

May Martha's father was a man hidden behind whiskers and spectacles. He lived for bugs and butterflies and all insects that fly or crawl or buzz or get down your back or in the butter. He was an etymologist, or words to that effect. He spent his life seining the air for flying fish of the June-bug order, and then sticking pins through 'em and calling 'em names.

He and May Martha were the whole family. He prized her highly as a fine specimen of the racibus humanus because she saw that he had food at times, and put his clothes on right side before, and kept his alcohol-bottles filled. Scientists, they say, are apt to be absent-minded.

There was another besides myself who thought May Martha Mangum one to be desired. That was Goodloe Banks, a young man just home from college. He had all the attainments to be found in books, Latin, Greek, philosophy, and especially the higher branches of mathematics and logic.

If it hadn't been for his habit of pouring out this information and learning on every one that he addressed, I'd have liked him pretty well. But, even as it was, he and I were, you would have thought, great pals.

We got together every time we could because each of us wanted to pump the other for whatever straws we could to find which way the wind blew from the heart of May Martha Mangum,rather a mixed metaphor; Goodloe Banks would never have been guilty of that. That is the way of rivals.

You might say that Goodloe ran to books, manners, culture, rowing, intellect, and clothes. I would have put you in mind more of baseball and Friday-night debating societies by way of culture and maybe of a good horseback rider.

But in our talks together, and in our visits and conversation with May Martha, neither Goodloe Banks nor I could find out which one of us she preferred. May Martha was a natural-born non-committal, and knew in her cradle how to keep people guessing.

As I said, old man Mangum was absentminded. After a long time he found out one day, a little butterfly must have told him-that two young men were trying to throw a net over the head of the young person, a daughter, or some such technical appendage, who looked after his comforts.

I never knew scientists could rise to such occasions. Old Mangum orally labelled and classified Goodloe and myself easily among the lowest orders of the vertebrates; and in English, too, without going any further into Latin than the simple references to Orgetorix, Rex Helvetii, which is as far as I ever went, myself. And he told us that if he ever caught us around his house again he would add us to his collection.

Goodloe Banks and I remained away five days, expecting the storm to subside. When we dared to call at the house again May Martha Mangum and her father were gone. Gone! The house they had rented was closed. Their little store of goods and chattels was gone also.

And not a word of farewell to either of us from May Martha, not a white, fluttering note pinned to the hawthorn-bush; not a chalk-mark on the gate-post nor a post-card in the post-office to give us a clew.

For two months Goodloe Banks and I, separately, tried every scheme we could think of to track the runaways. We used our friendship and influence with the ticket-agent, with livery-stable men, railroad conductors, and our one lone, lorn constable, but without results.

Then we became better friends and worse enemies than ever. We forgathered in the back room of Snyder's saloon every afternoon after work, and played dominoes, and laid conversational traps to find out from each other if anything had been discovered. That is the way of rivals.

Now, Goodloe Banks had a sarcastic way of displaying his own learning and putting me in the class that was reading "Poor Jane Ray, her bird is dead, she cannot play." Well, I rather liked Goodloe, and I had a contempt for his college learning, and I was always regarded as good-natured, so I kept my temper. And I was trying to find out if he knew anything about May Martha, so I endured his society.

In talking things over one afternoon he said to me:

"Suppose you do find her, Ed, whereby would you profit? Miss Mangum has a mind. Perhaps it is yet uncultured, but she is destined for higher things than you could give her. I have talked with no one who seemed to appreciate more the enchantment of the ancient poets and writers and the modern cults that have assimilated and expended their philosophy of life. Don't you think you are wasting your time looking for her?"

"My idea," said I, "of a happy home is an eight-room house in a grove of live-oaks by the side of a charco on a Texas prairie. A piano," I went on, "with an automatic player in the sitting-room, three thousand head of cattle under fence for a starter, a buckboard and ponies always hitched at a post for 'the missus 'and May Martha Mangum to spend the profits of the ranch as she pleases, and to abide with me, and put my slippers and pipe away every day in places where they cannot be found of evenings. That," said I, "is what is to be; and a fig - a dried, Smyrna, dago-stand fig - for your curriculums, cults, and philosophy."

"She is meant for higher things," repeated Goodloe Banks.

"Whatever she is meant for," I answered, just now she is out of pocket. And I shall find her as soon as I can without aid of the colleges."

"The game is blocked," said Goodloe, putting down a domino and we had the beer.

Shortly after that a young farmer whom I knew came into town and brought me a folded blue paper. He said his grandfather had just died. I concealed a tear, and he went on to say that the old man had jealously guarded this paper for twenty years. He left it to his family as part of his estate, the rest of which consisted of two mules and a hypotenuse of non-arable land.

The sheet of paper was of the old, blue kind used during the rebellion of the abolitionists against the secessionists. It was dated June 14, 1863, and it described the hiding-place of ten burro-loads of gold and silver coin valued at three hundred thousand dollars. Old Rundle, grandfather of his grandson, Sam, was given the information by a Spanish priest who was in on the treasure-burying, and who died many years before, no, afterward, in old Rundle's house. Old Rundle wrote it down from dictation.

"Why didn't your father look this up?" I asked young Rundle.

"He went blind before he could do so," he replied.

"Why didn't you hunt for it yourself?" I asked.

"Well," said he, "I've only known about the paper for ten years. First there was the spring ploughin' to do, and then choppin' the weeds out of the corn; and then come takin' fodder; and mighty soon winter was on us. It seemed to run along that way year after year."

That sounded perfectly reasonable to me, so I took it up with young Lee Rundle at once.

The directions on the paper were simple. The whole burro cavalcade laden with the treasure started from an old Spanish mission in Dolores County. They travelled due south by the compass until they reached the Alamito River. They forded this, and buried the treasure on the top of a little mountain shaped like a pack-saddle standing in a row between two higher ones. A heap of stones marked the place of the buried treasure. All the party except the Spanish priest were killed by Indians a few days later. The secret was a monopoly. It looked good to me.

Lee Rundle suggested that we rig out a camping outfit, hire a surveyor to run out the line from the Spanish mission, and then spend the three hundred thousand dollars seeing the sights in Fort Worth. But, without being highly educated, I knew a way to save time and expense.

We went to the State land-office and had a practical, what they call a "working," sketch made of all the surveys of land from the old mission to the Alamito River. On this map I drew a line due southward to the river. The length of lines of each survey and section of land was accurately given on the sketch. By these we found the point on the river and had a "connection" made with it and an important, well-identified corner of the Los Animos five-league survey, a grant made by King Philip of Spain.

By doing this we did not need to have the line run out by a surveyor. It was a great saving of expense and time.

So, Lee Rundle and I fitted out a two-horse wagon team with all the accessories, and drove a hundred and forty-nine miles to Chico, the nearest town to the point we wished to reach. There we picked up a deputy county surveyor. He found the corner of the Los Animos survey for us, ran out the five thousand seven hundred and twenty varas west that our sketch called for, laid a stone on the spot, had coffee and bacon, and caught the mail-stage back to Chico.

I was pretty sure we would get that three hundred thousand dollars. Lee Rundle's was to be only one-third, because I was paying all the expenses. With that two hundred thousand dollars I knew I could find May Martha Mangum if she was on earth. And with it I could flutter the butterflies in old man Mangum's dove-cot, too. If I could find that treasure!

But Lee and I established camp. Across the river were a dozen little mountains densely covered by cedar-brakes, but not one shaped like a pack-saddle. That did not deter us. Appearances are deceptive. A pack-saddle, like beauty, may exist only in the eye of the beholder.

I and the grandson of the treasure examined those cedar-covered hills with the care of a lady hunting for the wicked flea. We explored every side, top, circumference, mean elevation, angle, slope, and concavity of every one for two miles up and down the river. We spent four days doing so. Then we hitched up the roan and the dun, and hauled the remains of the coffee and bacon the one hundred and forty-nine miles back to Concho City.

Lee Rundle chewed much tobacco on the return trip. I was busy driving, because I was in a hurry.

As shortly as could be after our empty return Goodloe Banks and I forgathered in the back room of Snyder's saloon to play dominoes and fish for information. I told Goodloe about my expedition after the buried treasure.

"If I could have found that three hundred thousand dollars," I said to him, "I could have scoured and sifted the surface of the earth to find May Martha Mangum."

"She is meant for higher things," said Goodloe. "I shall find her myself. But, tell me how you went about discovering the spot where this unearthed increment was imprudently buried."

I told him in the smallest detail. I showed him the draughtsman's sketch with the distances marked plainly upon it.

After glancing over it in a masterly way, he leaned back in his chair and bestowed upon me an explosion of sardonic, superior, collegiate laughter.

"Well, you are a fool, Jim," he said, when he could speak.

"It's your play," said I, patiently, fingering my double-six.

"Twenty," said Goodloe, making two crosses on the table with his chalk.

"Why am I a fool?" I asked. "Buried treasure has been found before in many places."

"Because," said he, "in calculating the point on the river where your line would strike you neglected to allow for the variation. The variation there would be nine degrees west. Let me have your pencil."

Goodloe Banks figured rapidly on the back of an envelope.

"The distance, from north to south, of the line run from the Spanish mission," said he, "is exactly twenty-two miles. It was run by a pocket-compass, according to your story. Allowing for the variation, the point on the Alamito River where you should have searched for your treasure is exactly six miles and nine hundred and forty-five varas farther west than the place you hit upon. Oh, what a fool you are, Jim!"

"What is this variation that you speak of?" I asked. "I thought figures never lied."

"The variation of the magnetic compass," said Goodloe, "from the true meridian."

He smiled in his superior way; and then I saw come out in his face the singular, eager, consuming cupidity of the seeker after buried treasure.

"Sometimes," he said with the air of the oracle, "these old traditions of hidden money are not without foundation. Suppose you let me look over that paper describing the location. Perhaps together we might -"

The result was that Goodloe Banks and I, rivals in love, became companions in adventure. We went to Chico by stage from Huntersburg, the nearest railroad town. In Chico we hired a team drawing a covered spring-wagon and camping paraphernalia. We had the same surveyor run out our distance, as revised by Goodloe and his variations, and then dismissed him and sent him on his homeward road.

It was night when we arrived. I fed the horses and made a fire near the bank of the river and cooked supper. Goodloe would have helped, but his education had not fitted him for practical things.

But while I worked he cheered me with the expression of great thoughts handed down from the dead ones of old. He quoted some translations from the Greek at much length.

"Anacreon," he explained. "That was a favorite passage with Miss Mangum, as I recited it."

"She is meant for higher things," said I, repeating his phrase.

"Can there be anything higher," asked Goodloe, "than to dwell in the society of the classics, to live in the atmosphere of learning and culture? You have often decried education. What of your wasted efforts through your ignorance of simple mathematics? How soon would you have found your treasure if my knowledge had not shown you your error?"

"We'll take a look at those hills across the river first," said I, "and see what we find. I am still doubtful about variations. I have been brought up to believe that the needle is true to the pole."

The next morning was a bright June one. We were up early and had breakfast. Goodloe was charmed. He recited; Keats, I think it was, and Kelly or Shelley, while I broiled the bacon. We were getting ready to cross the river, which was little more than a shallow creek there, and explore the many sharp-peaked cedar-covered hills on the other side.

"My good Ulysses," said Goodloe, slapping me on the shoulder while I was washing the tin breakfast-plates, "let me see the enchanted document once more. I believe it gives directions for climbing the hill shaped like a pack-saddle. I never saw a pack-saddle. What is it like, Jim?"

"Score one against culture," said I. "I'll know it when I see it."

Goodloe was looking at old Rundle's document when he ripped out a most uncollegiate swear-word.

"Come here," he said, holding the paper up against the sunlight. "Look at that," he said, laying his finger against it.

On the blue paper, a thing I had never noticed before, I saw stand out in white letters the word and figures : "Malvern, 1898."

"What about it?" I asked.

"It's the water-mark," said Goodloe. "The paper was manufactured in 1898. The writing on the paper is dated 1863. This is a palpable fraud."

"Oh, I don't know," said I. "The Rundles are pretty reliable, plain, uneducated country people. Maybe the paper manufacturers tried to perpetrate a swindle."

And then Goodloe Banks went as wild as his education permitted. He dropped the glasses off his nose and glared at me.

"I've often told you you were a fool," he said. "You have let yourself be imposed upon by a clodhopper. And you have imposed upon me."

"How," I asked, "have I imposed upon you ?"

"By your ignorance," said he. "Twice I have discovered serious flaws in your plans that a common-school education should have enabled you to avoid. And," he continued, "I have been put to expense that I could ill afford in pursuing this swindling quest. I am done with it."

I rose and pointed a large pewter spoon at him, fresh from the dish-water.

"Goodloe Banks," I said, "I care not one parboiled navy bean for your education. I always barely tolerated it in any one, and I despised it in you. What has your learning done for you? It is a curse to yourself and a bore to your friends. Away," I said "away with your water-marks and variations! They are nothing to me. They shall not deflect me from the quest."

I pointed with my spoon across the river to a small mountain shaped like a pack-saddle.

"I am going to search that mountain," I went on, "for the treasure. Decide now whether you are in it or not. If you wish to let a water-mark or a variation shake your soul, you are no true adventurer. Decide."

A white cloud of dust began to rise far down the river road. It was the mail-wagon from Hesperus to Chico. Goodloe flagged it.

"I am done with the swindle," said he, sourly. "No one but a fool would pay any attention to that paper now. Well, you always were a fool, Jim. I leave you to your fate."

He gathered his personal traps, climbed into the mail-wagon, adjusted his glasses nervously, and flew away in a cloud of dust.

After I had washed the dishes and staked the horses on new grass, I crossed the shallow river and made my way slowly through the cedar-brakes up to the top of the hill shaped like a pack-saddle.

It was a wonderful June day. Never in my life had I seen so many birds, so many butter-flies, dragon-flies, grasshoppers, and such winged and stinged beasts of the air and fields.

I investigated the hill shaped like a pack-saddle from base to summit. I found an absolute absence of signs relating to buried treasure. There was no pile of stones, no ancient blazes on the trees, none of the evidences of the three hundred thousand dollars, as set forth in the document of old man Rundle.

I came down the hill in the cool of the afternoon. Suddenly, out of the cedar-brake I stepped into a beautiful green valley where a tributary small stream ran into the Alamito River.

And there I was started to see what I took to be a wild man, with unkempt beard and ragged hair, pursuing a giant butterfly with brilliant wings.

"Perhaps he is an escaped madman," I thought; and wondered how he had
strayed so far from seats of education and learning.

And then I took a few more steps and saw a vine-covered cottage near the small stream. And in a little grassy glade I saw May Martha Mangum plucking wild flowers.

She straightened up and looked at me. For the first time since I knew her I saw her face, which was the color of the white keys of a new piano - turn pink. I walked toward her without a word. She let the gathered flowers trickle slowly from her hand to the grass.

"I knew you would come, Jim," she said clearly. "Father wouldn't let me write, but I knew you would come.

What followed you may guess, there was my wagon and team just across the river.

I've often wondered what good too much education is to a man if he can't use it for himself. If all the benefits of it are to go to others, where does it come in?

For May Martha Mangum abides with me. There is an eight-room house in a live-oak grove, and a piano with an automatic player, and a good start toward the three thousand head of cattle is under fence.

And when I ride home at night my pipe and slippers are put away in places where they cannot be found.

But who cares for that? Who cares, who cares?

TO HIM WHO WAITS

The Hermit of the Hudson was hustling about his cave with unusual animation.

The cave was on or in the top of a little spur of the Catskills that had strayed down to the river's edge, and, not having a ferry ticket, had to stop there. The bijou mountains were densely wooded and were infested by ferocious squirrels and woodpeckers that forever menaced the summer transients. Like a badly sewn strip of white braid, a macadamized road ran between the green skirt of the hills and the foamy lace of the river's edge. A dim path wound from the comfortable road up a rocky height to the hermit's cave. One mile upstream was the Viewpoint Inn, to which summer folk from the city came; leaving cool, electric-fanned apartments that they might be driven about in burning sunshine, shrieking, in gasoline launches, by spindle-legged Modreds bearing the blankest of shields.

Train your lorgnette upon the hermit and let your eye receive the personal touch that shall endear you to the hero.

A man of forty, judging him fairly, with long hair curling at the ends, dramatic eyes, and a forked brown beard like those that were imposed upon the West some years ago by self-appointed "divine healers" who succeeded the grasshopper crop. His outward vesture appeared to be kind of gunny-sacking cut and made into a garment that would have made the fortune of a London tailor. His long, well-shaped fingers, delicate nose, and poise of manner raised him high above the class of hermits who fear water and bury money in oyster-cans in their caves in spots indicated by rude crosses chipped in the stone wall above.

The hermit's home was not altogether a cave. The cave was an addition to the hermitage, which was a rude hut made of poles daubed with clay and covered with the best quality of rust-proof zinc roofing.

In the house proper there were stone slabs for seats, a rustic bookcase made of unplaned poplar planks, and a table formed of a wooden slab laid across two upright pieces of granite, something between the furniture of a Druid temple and that of a Broadway beefsteak dungeon. Hung against the walls were skins of wild animals purchased in the vicinity of Eighth Street and University Place, New York.

The rear of the cabin merged into the cave. There the hermit cooked his meals on a rude stone hearth. With infinite patience and an old axe he had chopped natural shelves in the rocky walls. On them stood his stores of flour, bacon, lard, talcum-powder, kerosene, baking-powder, soda-mint tablets, pepper, salt, and Olivo-Cremo Emulsion for chaps and roughness of the hands and face.

The hermit had hermited there for ten years. He was an asset of the Viewpoint Inn. To its guests he was second in interest only to the Mysterious Echo in the Haunted Glen. And the Lover's Leap beat him only a few inches, flat-footed. He was known far (but not very wide, on account of the topography) as a. scholar of brilliant intellect who had forsworn the world because he had been jilted in a love affair. Every Saturday night the Viewpoint Inn sent to him surreptitiously a basket of provisions. He never left the immediate outskirts of his hermitage. Guests of the inn who visited him said his store of knowledge, wit, and scintillating philosophy were simply wonderful, you know.

That summer the Viewpoint Inn was crowded with guests. So, on Saturday nights, there were extra cans of tomatoes, and sirloin steak, instead of "rounds," in the hermit's basket.

Now you have the material allegations in the case. So, make way for Romance.

Evidently the hermit expected a visitor. He carefully combed his long hair and parted his apostolic beard. When the ninety-eight-cent alarm-clock on a stone shelf announced the hour of five he picked up his gunny-sacking skirts, brushed them carefully, gathered an oaken staff, and strolled slowly into the thick woods that surrounded the hermitage.

He had not long to wait. Up the faint pathway, slippery with its carpet of pine-needles, toiled Beatrix, youngest and fairest of the famous Trenholme sisters. She was all in blue from hat to canvas pumps, varying in tint from the shade of the tinkle of a bluebell at daybreak on a spring Saturday to the deep hue of a Monday morning at nine when the washer-woman has failed to show up.

Beatrix dug her cerulean parasol deep into the pine-needles and sighed. The hermit, on the q. t., removed a grass burr from the ankle of one sandalled foot with the big toe of his other one.

She blued, and almost starched and ironed him, with her cobalt eyes.

"It must be so nice," she said in little, tremulous gasps, "to be a hermit, and have ladies climb mountains to talk to you."

The hermit folded his arms and leaned against a tree. Beatrix, with a sigh, settled down upon the mat of pine-needles like a bluebird upon her nest. The hermit followed suit; drawing his feet rather awkwardly under his gunny-sacking.

"It must be nice to be a mountain," said he, with ponderous lightness, "and have angels in blue climb up you instead of flying over you."

"Mamma had neuralgia," said Beatrix, "and went to bed, or I couldn't have come. It's dreadfully hot at that horrid old inn. But we hadn't the money to go anywhere else this summer."

"Last night," said the hermit, "I climbed to the top of that big rock above us. I could see the lights of the inn and hear a strain or two of the music when the wind was right. I imagined you moving gracefully in the arms of others to the dreamy music of the waltz amid the fragrance of flowers. Think how lonely I must have been!"

The youngest, handsomest, and poorest of the famous Trenholme sisters sighed.

"You haven't quite hit it," she said, plaintively. "I was moving gracefully at the arms of another. Mamma had one of her periodical attacks of rheumatism in both elbows and shoulders, and I had to rub them for an hour with that horrid old liniment. I hope you didn't think that smelled like flowers. You know, there were some West Point boys and a yachtload of young men from the city at last evening's weekly dance. I've known mamma to sit by an open window for three hours with one-half of her registering 85 degrees and the other half frostbitten, and never sneeze once. But just let a bunch of ineligibles come around where I am, and she'll begin to swell at the knuckles and shriek with pain. And I have to take her to her room and rub her arms. To see mamma dressed you'd be surprised to know the number of square inches of surface there are to her arms. I think it must be delightful to be a hermit. That, cassock, gabardine, isn't it? that you wear is so becoming. Do you make it, or them, of course you must have changes- yourself? And what a blessed relief it must be to wear sandals instead of shoes! Think how we must suffer, no matter how small I buy my shoes they always pinch my toes. Oh, why can't there be lady hermits, too!"

The beautifulest and most adolescent Trenholme sister extended two slender blue ankles that ended in two enormous blue-silk bows that almost concealed two fairy Oxfords, also of one of the forty-seven shades of blue. The hermit, as if impelled by a kind of reflex-telepathic action, drew his bare toes farther beneath his gunny-sacking.

"I have heard about the romance of your life," said Miss Trenholme, softly. "They have it printed on the back of the menu card at the inn. Was she very beautiful and charming?"

"On the bills of fare!" muttered the hermit; "but what do I care for the world's babble? Yes, she was of the highest and grandest type. Then," he continued, "then I thought the world could never contain another equal to her. So I forsook it and repaired to this mountain fastness to spend the remainder of my life alone to devote and dedicate my remaining years to her memory."

"It's grand," said Miss Trenholme, "absolutely grand. I think a hermit's life is the ideal one. No bill-collectors calling, no dressing for dinner, how I'd like to be one! But there's no such luck for me. If I don't marry this season I honestly believe mamma will force me into settlement work or trimming hats. It isn't because I'm getting old or ugly; but we haven't enough money left to butt in at any of the swell places any more. And I don't want to marry, unless it's somebody I like. That's why I'd like to be a hermit. Hermits don't ever marry, do they ?"

"Hundreds of 'em," said the hermit, "when they've found the right one."

"But they're hermits," said the youngest and beautifulest, "because they've lost the right one, aren't they?"

"Because they think they have," answered the recluse, fatuously. "Wisdom comes to one in a mountain cave as well as to one in the world of 'swells,' as I believe they are called in the argot."

"When one of the 'swells' brings it to them," said Miss Trenholme. "And my folks are swells. That's the trouble. But there are so many swells at the seashore in the summer-time that we hardly amount to more than ripples. So we've had to put all our money into river and harbor appropriations. We were all girls, you know. There were four of us. I'm the only surviving one. The others have been married off. All to money. Mamma is so proud of my sisters. They send her the loveliest pen-wipers and art calendars every Christmas. I'm the only one on the market now. I'm forbidden to look at any one who hasn't money."

"But -" began the hermit.

"But, oh," said the beautifulest "of course hermits have great pots of gold and doubloons buried somewhere near three great oak-trees. They all have."

"I have not," said the hermit, regretfully.

"I'm so sorry," said Miss Trenholme. "I always thought they had. I think I must go now."

Oh, beyond question, she was the beautifulest.

"Fair lady -" began the hermit.

"I am Beatrix Trenholme, some call me Trix," she said. "You must come to the inn to see me."

"I haven't been a stone's, throw from my cave in ten years," said the hermit.

"You must come to see me there," she repeated. "Any evening except Thursday."

The hermit smiled weakly.

"Good-bye," she said, gathering the folds of her pale-blue skirt. "I shall expect you. But not on Thursday evening, remember."

What an interest it would give to the future menu cards of the Viewpoint Inn to have these printed lines added to them: "Only once during the more than ten years of his lonely existence did the mountain hermit leave his famous cave. That was when he was irresistibly drawn to the inn by the fascinations of Miss Beatrix Trenholme, youngest and most beautiful of the celebrated Trenholme sisters, whose brilliant marriage to -"

Aye, to whom?

The hermit walked back to the hermitage. At the door stood Bob Binkley, his old friend and companion of the days before he had renounced the world, Bob, himself, arrayed like the orchids of the greenhouse in the summer man's polychromatic garb,Bob, the millionaire, with his fat, firm, smooth, shrewd face, his diamond rings, sparkling fob-chain, and pleated bosom. He was two years older than the hermit, and looked five years younger.

"You're Hamp Ellison, in spite of those whiskers and that going-away bathrobe," he shouted. "I read about you on the bill of fare at the inn. They've run your biography in between the cheese and 'Not Responsible for Coats and Umbrellas.' What 'd you do it for, Hamp? And ten years, too - geewhilikins!"

"You're just the same," said the hermit. "Come in and sit down. Sit on that limestone rock over there; it's softer than the granite."

"I can't understand it, old man," said Binkley. "I can see how you could give up a woman for ten years, but not ten years for a woman. Of course I know why you did it. Everybody does. Edith Carr. She jilted four or five besides you. But you were the only one who took to a hole in the ground. The others had recourse to whiskey, the Klondike, politics, and that similia similibus cure. But, say, Hamp, Edith Carr was just about the finest woman in the world, high-toned and proud and noble, and playing her ideals to win at all kinds of odds. She certainly was a crackerjack."

"After I renounced the world," said the hermit, "I never heard of her again."

"She married me," said Binkley.

The hermit leaned against the wooden walls of his ante-cave and wriggled his toes.

"I know how you feel about it," said Binkley. "What else could she do? There were her four sisters and her mother and old man Carr, you remember how he put all the money he had into dirigible balloons? Well, everything was coming down and nothing going up with 'em, as you might say. Well, I know Edith as well as you do, although I married her. I was worth a million then, but I've run it up since to between five and six. It wasn't me she wanted as much as, well, it was about like this. She had that bunch on her hands, and they had to be taken care of. Edith married me two months after you did the ground-squirrel act. I thought she liked me, too, at the time."

"And now?" inquired the recluse.

"We're better friends than ever now. She got a divorce from me two years ago. Just incompatibility. I didn't put in any defence. Well, well, well, Hamp, this is certainly a funny dugout you've built here. But you always were a hero of fiction. Seems like you'd have been the very one to strike Edith's fancy. Maybe you did, but it's the bank - roll that catches 'em, my boy, your caves and whiskers won't do it. Honestly, Hamp, don't you think you've been a darned fool?"

The hermit smiled behind his tangled beard. He was and always had been so superior to the crude and mercenary Binkley that even his vulgarities could not anger him. Moreover, his studies and meditations in his retreat had raised him far above the little vanities of the world. His little mountain-side had been almost an Olympus, over the edge of which he saw, smiling, the bolts hurled in the valleys of man below. Had his ten years of renunciation, of thought, of devotion to an ideal, of living scorn of a sordid world, been in vain? Up from the world had come to him the youngest and beautifulest, fairer than Edith, one and three-seventh times lovelier than the seven-years-served Rachel. So the hermit smiled in his beard.

When Binkley had relieved the hermitage from the blot of his presence and the first faint star showed above the pines, the hermit got the can of baking-powder from his cupboard. He still smiled behind his beard.

There was a slight rustle in the doorway. There stood Edith Carr, with all the added beauty and stateliness and noble bearing that ten years had brought her.

She was never one to chatter. She looked at the hermit with her large, thinking, dark eyes. The hermit stood still, surprised into a pose as motionless as her own. Only his subconscious sense of the fitness of things caused him to turn the baking-powder can slowly in his hands until its red label was hidden against his bosom.

"I am stopping at the inn," said Edith, in low but clear tones. "I heard of you there. I told myself that I must see you. I want to ask your forgiveness. I sold my happiness for money. There were others to be provided for but that does not excuse me. I just wanted to see you and ask your forgiveness. You have lived here ten years, they tell me, cherishing my memory! I was blind, Hampton. I could not see then that all the money in the world cannot weigh in the scales against a faithful heart. If - but it is too late now, of course."

Her assertion was a question clothed as best it could be in a loving woman's pride. But through the thin disguise the hermit saw easily that his lady had come back to him, if he chose. He had won a golden crown, if it pleased him to take it. The reward of his decade of faithfulness was ready for his hand if he desired to stretch it forth.

For the space of one minute the old enchantment shone upon him with a reflected radiance. And then by turns he felt the manly sensations of indignation at having been discarded, and of repugnance at having been - as it were - sought again. And last of all how strange that it should have come at last! the pale-blue vision of the beautifulest of the Trenholme sisters illuminated his mind's eye and left him without a waver.

"It is too late," he said, in deep tones, pressing the baking-powder can against his heart.

Once she turned after she had gone slowly twenty yards down the path. The hermit had begun to twist the lid off his can, but he hid it again under his sacking robe. He could see her great eyes shining sadly through the twilight; but he stood inflexible in the doorway of his shack and made no sign.

Just as the moon rose on Thursday evening the hermit was seized by the world-madness.

Up from the inn, fainter than the horns of elf-land, came now and then a few bars of music played by the casino band. The Hudson was broadened by the night into an illimitable sea, those lights, dimly seen on its opposite shore, were not beacons for prosaic trolley-lines, but low-set stars millions of miles away. The waters in front of the inn were gay with fireflies or were they motor-boats, smelling of gasoline and oil? Once the hermit had known these things and had sported with Amaryllis in the shade of the red-and-white-striped awnings. But for ten years he had turned a heedless ear to these far-off echoes of a frivolous world. But to-night there was something wrong.

The casino band was playing a waltz - a waltz. What a fool he had been to tear deliberately ten years of his life from the calendar of existence for one who had given him up for the false joys that wealth "tum ti tum ti tum ti" how did that waltz go? But those years had not been sacrificed - had they not brought him the star and pearl of all the world, the youngest and beautifulest of –

"But do not come on Thursday evening," she had insisted. Perhaps by now she would be moving slowly and gracefully to the strains of that waltz, held closely by West-Pointers or city commuters, while he, who had read in her eyes things that had recompensed him for ten lost years of life, moped like some wild animal in its mountain den. Why should -"

"Damn it," said the hermit, suddenly, "I'll do it!"

He threw down his Marcus Aurelius and threw off his gunny-sack toga. he dragged a dust-covered trunk from a corner of the cave, and with difficulty wrenched open its lid.

Candles he had in plenty, and the cave was soon aglow. Clothes - ten years old in cut - scissors, razors, hats, shoes, all his discarded attire and belongings, were dragged ruthlessly from their renunciatory rest and strewn about in painful disorder.

A pair of scissors soon reduced his beard sufficiently for the dulled razors to perform approximately their office. Cutting his own hair was beyond the hermit's skill. So he only combed and brushed it backward as smoothly as he could. Charity forbids us to consider the heartburnings and exertions of one so long removed from haberdashery and society.

At the last the hermit went to an inner corner of his cave and began to dig in the soft earth with a long iron spoon. Out of the cavity he thus made he drew a tin can, and out of the can three thousand dollars in bills, tightly rolled and wrapped in oiled silk. He was a real hermit, as this may assure you.

You may take a brief look at him as he hastens down the little mountain-side. A long, wrinkled black frock-coat reached to his calves. White duck trousers, unacquainted with the tailor's goose, a pink shirt, white standing collar with brilliant blue butterfly tie, and buttoned congress gaiters. But think, sir and madam - ten years!

From beneath a narrow-brimmed straw hat with a striped band flowed his hair. Seeing him, with all your shrewdness you could not have guessed him. You would have said that he played Hamlet or the tuba or pinochle, you would never have laid your hand on your heart and said:

"He is a hermit who lived ten years in a cave for love of one lady - to win another."

The dancing pavilion extended above the waters of the river. Gay lanterns and frosted electric globes shed a soft glamour within it. A hundred ladies and gentlemen from the inn and summer cottages flitted in and about it. To the left of the dusty roadway down which the hermit had tramped were the inn and grill-room. Something seemed to be on there, too. The windows were brilliantly lighted, and music was playing, music different from the two-steps and waltzes of the casino band.

A negro man wearing a white jacket came through the iron gate, with its immense granite posts and wrought-iron lamp-holders.

"What is going on here to-night?" asked the hermit.

"Well, sah," said the servitor, "dey is having de reg'lar Thursday-evenin' dance in de casino. And in de grill-room dere's a beefsteak dinner, sah."

The hermit glanced up at the inn on the hillside whence burst suddenly a triumphant strain of splendid harmony.

"And up there," said he, "they are playing Mendelssohn, what is going on up there?"

"Up in de inn," said the dusky one, "dey is a weddin' goin' on. Mr. Binkley, a mighty rich man, am marryin' Miss Trenholme, sah - de young lady who am quite de belle of de place, sah."

HE ALSO SERVES

If I could have a thousand years, just one little thousand years more of life, I might, in that time, draw near enough to true Romance to touch the hem of her robe.

Up from ships men come, and from waste places and forest and road and garret and cellar to maunder to me in strangely distributed words of the things they have seen and considered. The recording of their tales is no more than a matter of ears and fingers. There are only two fates I dread, deafness and writer's cramp. The hand is yet steady; let the ear bear the blame if these printed words be not in the order they were delivered to me by Hunky Magee, true camp-follower of fortune.

Biography shall claim you but an instant, I first knew Hunky when he was head-waiter at Chubb's little beefsteak restaurant and cafe on Third Avenue. There was only one waiter besides.

Then, successively, I caromed against him in the little streets of the Big City after his trip to Alaska, his voyage as cook with a treasure-seeking expedition to the Caribbean, and his failure as a pearl-fisher in the Arkansas River. Between these dashes into the land of adventure he usually came back to Chubb's for a while. Chubb's was a port for him when gales blew too high; but when you dined there and Hunky went for your steak you never knew whether he would come to anchor in the kitchen or in the Malayan Archipelago. You wouldn't care for his description, he was soft of voice and hard of face, and rarely had to use more than one eye to quell any approach to a disturbance among Chubb's customers.

One night I found Hunky standing at a corner of Twenty-third Street and Third Avenue after an absence of several months. In ten minutes we had a little round table between us in a quiet corner, and my ears began to get busy. I leave out my sly ruses and feints to draw Hunky's word-of-mouth blows, it all came to something like this:

"Speaking of the next election," said Hunky, "did you ever know much about Indians? No? I don't mean the Cooper, Beadle, cigar-store, or Laughing Water kind-I mean the modern Indian, the kind that takes Greek prizes in colleges and scalps the half-back on the other side in football games. The kind that eats macaroons and tea in the afternoons with the daughter of the professor of biology, and fills up on grasshoppers and fried rattlesnake when they get back to the ancestral wickiup.

"Well, they ain't so bad. I like 'em better than most foreigners that have come over in the last few hundred years. One thing about the Indian is this: when he mixes with the white race he swaps all his own vices for them of the pale-faces and he retains all his own virtues. Well, his virtues are enough to call out the reserves whenever he lets 'em loose. But the imported foreigners adopt our virtues and keep their own vices and it's going to take our whole standing army some day to police that gang.

"But let me tell you about the trip I took to Mexico with High jack Snakefeeder, a Cherokee twice removed, a graduate of a Pennsylvania college and the latest thing in pointed-toed, rubber-heeled, patent kid moccasins and Madras hunting-shirt with turned-back cuffs. He was a friend of mine. I met him in Tahlequah when I was out there during the land boom, and we got thick. He had got all there was out of colleges and had come back to lead his people out of Egypt. He was a man of first-class style and wrote essays, and had been invited to visit rich guys' houses in Boston and such places.

"There was a Cherokee girl in Muscogee that High Jack was foolish about. He took me to see her a few times. Her name was Florence Blue Feather but you want to clear your mind of all ideas of squaws with nose-rings and army blankets. This young lady was whiter than you are, and better educated than I ever was. You couldn't have told her from any of the girls shopping in the swell Third Avenue stores. I liked her so well that, I got to calling on her now and then when High Jack wasn't along, which is the way of friends in such matters. She was educated at the Muscogee College, and was making a specialty of - let's see – eth - yes, ethnology. That's the art that goes back and traces the descent of different races of people, leading up from jelly-fish through monkeys and to the O'Briens. High Jack had took up that line too, and had read papers about it before all kinds of riotous assemblies; Chautauquas and Choctaws and chowder-parties, and such. Having a mutual taste for musty information like that was what made 'em like each other, I suppose. But I don't know! What they call congeniality of tastes ain't always it. Now, when Miss Blue Feather and me was talking together, I listened to her affidavits about the first families of the Land of Nod being cousins german (well, if the Germans don't nod, who does?) to the mound-builders of Ohio with incomprehension and respect. And when I'd tell her about the Bowery and Coney Island, and sing her a few songs that I'd heard the Jamaica niggers sing at their church lawn-parties, she didn't look much less interested than she did when High Jack would tell her that he had a pipe that the first inhabitants of America originally arrived here on stilts after a freshet at Tenafly, New Jersey.

"But I was going to tell you more about High Jack.

"About six months ago I get a letter from him, saying he'd been commissioned by the Minority Report Bureau of Ethnology at Washington to go down to Mexico and translate some excavations or dig up the meaning of some shorthand notes on some ruins or something of that sort. And if I'd go along he could squeeze the price into the expense account.

"Well, I'd been holding a napkin over my arm at Chubb's about long enough then, so I wired High Jack 'Yes'; and he sent me a ticket, and I met him in Washington, and he had a lot of news to tell me. First of all, was that Florence Blue Feather had suddenly disappeared from her home and environments.

"'Run away?' I asked.

"'Vanished,' says High Jack. 'Disappeared like your shadow when the sun goes under a cloud. She was seen on the street, and then she turned a corner and nobody ever seen her afterward. The whole community turned out to look for her, but we never found a clew.'

"'That's bad,that's bad,' says I. 'She was a mighty nice girl, and as smart as you find em.

"High Jack seemed to take it hard. I guess he must have esteemed Miss Blue Feather quite highly. I could see that he'd referred the matter to the whiskey-jug. That was his weak point and many another man's. I've noticed that when a man loses a girl he generally takes to drink either just before or just after it happens.

"From Washington we railroaded it to New Orleans, and there took a tramp steamer bound for Belize. And a gale pounded us all down the Caribbean, and nearly wrecked us on the Yucatan coast opposite a little town without a harbor called Boca de Coacoyula. Suppose the ship had run against that name in the dark!

"'Better fifty years of Europe than a cyclone in the bay,' says High

Jack Snakefeeder. So we get the captain to send us ashore in a dory when the squall seemed to cease from squalling.

"'We will find ruins here or make 'em,' says High. 'The Government doesn't care which we do. An appropriation is an appropriation.'

"Boca de Coacoyula was a dead town. Them biblical towns we read About, Tired and Siphon, after they was destroyed, they must have looked like Forty-second Street and Broadway compared to this Boca place. It still claimed 1300 inhabitants as estimated and engraved on the stone court-house by the census-taker in 1597. The citizens were a mixture of Indians and other Indians; but some of 'em was light-colored, which I was surprised to see. The town was huddled up on the shore, with woods so thick around it that a subpoena-server couldn't have reached a monkey ten yards away with the papers. We wondered what kept it from being annexed to Kansas; but we soon found out that it was Major Bing.

"Major Bing was the ointment around the fly. He had the cochineal, sarsaparilla, log-wood, annatto, hemp, and all other dye-woods and pure food adulteration concessions cornered. He had five-sixths of the Boca de Thingama jiggers working for him on shares. It was a beautiful graft. We used to brag about Morgan and E. H. and others of our wisest when I was in the provinces but now no more. That peninsula has got our little country turned into a submarine without even the observation tower showing.

"Major Bing's idea was this. He had the population go forth into the forest and gather these products. When they brought 'em in he gave 'em one-fifth for their trouble. Sometimes they'd strike and demand a sixth. The Major always gave in to 'em.

"The Major had a bungalow so close on the sea that the nine-inch tide seeped through the cracks in the kitchen floor. Me and him and High Jack Snakefeeder sat on the porch and drank rum from noon till midnight. He said he had piled up $300,000 in New Orleans banks, and High and me could stay with him forever if we would. But High Jack happened to think of the United States, and began to talk ethnology.

"'Ruins!' says Major Bing. 'The woods are full of 'em. I don't know how far they date back, but they was here before I came.'

"High Jack asks what form of worship the citizens of that locality are addicted to.

"'Why,' says the Major, rubbing his nose, 'I can't hardly say. I imagine it's infidel or Aztec or Nonconformist or something like that.

There's a church here, a Methodist or some other kind, with a parson named Skidder. He claims to have converted the people to Christianity. He and me don't assimilate except on state occasions. I imagine they worship some kind of gods or idols yet. But Skidder says he has 'em in the fold.'

"A few days later High Jack and me, prowling around, strikes a plain path into the forest, and follows it a good four miles. Then a branch turns to the left. We go a mile, maybe, down that, and run up against the finest ruin you ever saw, solid stone with trees and vines and under-brush all growing up against it and in it and through it. All over it was chiselled carvings of funny beasts and people that would have been arrested if they'd ever come out in vaudeville that way. We approached it from the rear.

"High Jack had been drinking too much rum ever since we landed in Boca. You know how an Indian is - the palefaces fixed his clock when they introduced him to firewater. He'd brought a quart along with him.

"'Hunky,' says he, 'we'll explore the ancient temple. It may be that the storin that landed us here was propitious. The Minority Report Bureau of Ethnology,' says he, 'may yet profit by the vagaries of wind and tide.'

"We went in the rear door of the bum edifice. We struck a kind of alcove without bath. There was a granite davenport, and a stone wash-stand without any soap or exit for the water, and some hardwood pegs drove into holes in the wall, and that was all. To go out of that furnished apartment into a Harlem hall bedroom would make you feel like getting back home from an amateur violoncello solo at an East Side Settlement house.

"While High was examining some hieroglyphics on the wall that the stone-masons must have made when their tools slipped, I stepped into the front room. That was at least thirty by fifty feet, stone floor, six little windows like square port-holes that didn't let much light in.

"I looked back over my shoulder, and sees High Jack's face three feet away.

"'High,' says I, 'of all the -'

"And then I noticed he looked funny, and I turned around.

"He'd taken off his clothes to the waist, and he didn't seem to hear me. I touched him, and came near beating it. High Jack had turned to stone. I had been drinking some rum myself.

"'Ossified!' I says to him, loudly. 'I knew what would happen if you kept it up.'

"And then High Jack comes in from the alcove when he hears me conversing with nobody, and we have a look at Mr. Snakefeeder No. 2. It's a stone idol, or god, or revised statute or something, and it looks as much like High Jack as one green pea looks like itself. It's got exactly his face and size and color, but it's steadier on its pins. It stands on a kind of rostrum or pedestal, and you can see it's been there ten million years.

"'He's a cousin of mine,' sings High, and then he turns solemn.

"'Hunky,' he says, putting one hand on my shoulder and one on the statue's, 'I'm in the holy temple of my ancestors.'

"'Well, if looks goes for anything,' says I, 'you've struck a twin. Stand side by side with buddy, and let's see if there's any diff'erence.'

"There wasn't. You know an Indian can keep his face as still as an iron dog's when he wants to, so when High Jack froze his features you couldn't have told him from the other one.

"'There's some letters,' says I, 'on his nob's pedestal, but I can't make 'em out. The alphabet of this country seems to be composed of sometimes a, e, I, o, and u, but generally z's, l's, and t's.'

"High Jack's ethnology gets the upper hand of his rum for a minute, and he investigates the inscription.

"'Hunky,' says he, 'this is a statue of Tlotopaxl, one of the most powerful gods of the ancient Aztecs.'

"'Glad to know him,' says I, 'but in his present condition he reminds me of the joke Shakespeare got off on Julius Caesar. We might say about your friend:

"'Imperious what's-his-name, dead and tunied to stone
No use to write or call him on the 'phone.'

"'Hunky,' says High Jack Snakefeeder, looking at me funny, 'do you believe in reincarnation?'

"'It sounds to me,' says I, 'like either a clean-up of the slaughter-houses or a new kind of Boston pink. I don't know.'

"'I believe,' says he, 'that I am the reincarnation of Tlotopaxl. My researches have convinced me that the Cherokees, of all the North American tribes, can boast of the straightest descent from the proud Aztec race. That,' says he, 'was a favorite theory of mine and Florence Blue Feather's. And she, what' if she -!'

"High Jack grabs my arm and walls his eyes at me. Just then he looked more like his eminent co-Indian murderer, Crazy Horse.

"'Well,' says I, 'what if she, what if she, what if she? You're drunk,' says I. 'Impersonating idols and believing in, what was it? recarnalization? Let's have a drink,' says I. 'It's as spooky here as a Brooklyn artificial-limb factory at midnight with the gas turned down.'

"Just then I heard somebody coming, and I dragged High Jack into the bedless bedchamber. There was peep-holes bored through the wall, so we could see the whole front part of the temple.

Major Bing told me afterward that the ancient priests in charge used to rubber through them at the congregation.

"In a few minutes an old Indian woman came in with a' big oval earthen dish full of grub. She set it on a square block of stone in front of the graven image, and laid down and walloped her face on the floor a few times, and then took a walk for herself.

"High Jack and me was hungry, so we came out and looked it over. There was goat steaks and fried rice-cakes, and plantains and cassava, and broiled land-crabs and mangoes, nothing like what you get at Chubb's.

"We ate hearty and had another round of rum.

"'It must be old Tecumseh's, or whatever you call him, birthday,' says I. 'Or do they feed him every day? I thought gods only drank vanilla on Mount Catawampus.'

"Then some more native parties in short kimonos that showed their aboriginees punctured the near-horizon, and me and High had to skip back into Father Axletree's private boudoir. They came by ones, twos, and threes, and left all sorts of offerings, there was enough grub for Bingham's nine gods of war, with plenty left over for the Peace Conference at The Hague. They brought jars of honey, and bunches of bananas, and bottles of wine, and stacks of tortillas, and beautiful shawls worth one hundred dollars apiece that the Indian women weave of a kind of vegetable fibre like silk. All of 'em got down and wriggled on the floor in front of that hard-finish god, and then sneaked off through the woods again.

"'I wonder who gets this rake-off?' remarks High Jack.

"'Oh,' says I, 'there's priests or deputy idols or a committee of disarrangements somewhere in the woods on the job. Wherever you find a god you'll find somebody waiting to take charge of the burnt offerings.'

"And then we took another swig of rum and walked out to the parlor front door to cool off, for it was as hot inside as a summer camp on the Palisades.

"And while we stood there in the breeze we looks down the path and sees a young lady approaching the blasted ruin. She was bare-footed and had on a white robe, and carried a wreath of white flowers in her hand. When she got nearer we saw she had a long blue feather stuck through her black hair. And when she got nearer still me and High Jack Snakefeeder grabbed each other to keep from tumbling down on the floor; for the girl's face was as much like Florence Blue Feather's as his was like old King Toxicology's.

"And then was when High Jack's booze drowned his system of ethnology. He dragged me inside back of the statue, and says:

"'Lay hold of it, Hunky. We'll pack it into the other room. I felt it all the time,' says he. 'I'm the reconsideration of the god Locomotorataxia, and Florence Blue Feather was my bride a thousand years ago. She has come to seek me in the temple where I used to reign.'

"'All right,' says I. 'There's no use arguing against the rum question. You take his feet.'

"We lifted the three-hundred-pound stone god, and carried him into the back room of the cafe, the temple, I mean,and leaned him against the wall. It was more work than bouncing three live ones from an all-night Broadway joint on New-Year's Eve.

"Then High Jack ran out and brought in a couple of them Indian silk shawls and began to undress himself.

"'Oh, figs!' says I. 'Is it thus? Strong drink is an adder and subtractor, too. Is it the heat or the call of the wild that's got you ?'

"But High Jack is too full of exaltation and cane-juice to reply. He stops the disrobing business just short of the Manhattan Beach rules, and then winds them red-and-white shawls around him, and goes out and stands on the pedestal as steady as any platinum deity you ever saw. And I looks through a peek-hole to see what he is up to.

"In a few minutes in comes the girl with the flower wreath. Danged if I wasn't knocked a little silly when she got close, she looked so exactly much like Florence Blue Feather. 'I wonder,' says I to myself, 'if she has been reincarcerated, too? If I could see,' says I to myself, 'whether she has a mole on her left-' But the next minute I thought she looked one-eighth of a shade darker than Florence; but she looked good at that. And High Jack hadn't drunk all the rum that had been drank.

"The girl went up within ten feet of the bum idol, and got down and massaged her nose with the floor, like the rest did. Then she went nearer and laid the flower wreath on the block of stone at High Jack's feet. Rummy as I was, I thought it was kind of nice of her to think of offering flowers instead of household and kitchen provisions. Even a stone god ought to appreciate a little sentiment like that on top of the fancy groceries they had piled up in front of him.

"And then High Jack steps down from his pedestal, quiet, and mentions a few words that sounded just like the hieroglyphics carved on the walls of the ruin. The girl gives a little jump backward, and her eyes fly open as big as doughnuts; but she don't beat it.

"Why didn't she? I'll tell you why I think why. It don't seem to a girl so supernatural, unlikely, strange, and startling that a stone god should come to life for her. If he was to do it for one of them snub-nosed brown girls on the other side of the woods, now, it would be different, but her! I'll bet she said to herself:

'Well, goodness me! you've been a long time getting on your job. I've half a mind not to speak to you.'

"But she and High Jack holds hands and walks away out of the temple together. By the time I'd had time to take another drink and enter upon the scene they was twenty yards away, going up the path in the woods that the girl had come down. With the natural scenery already in place, it was just like a play to watch 'em, she looking up at him, and him giving her back the best that an Indian can hand, out in the way of a goo-goo eye. But there wasn't anything in that recarnification and revulsion to tintype for me.

"'Hey! Injun!' I yells out to High Jack.

'We've got a board-bill due in town, and you're leaving me without a cent. Brace up and cut out the Neapolitan fisher-maiden, and let's go back home.'

"But on the two goes; without looking once back until, as you might say, the forest swallowed 'em up. And I never saw or heard of High Jack Snakefeeder from that day to this. I don't know if the Cherokees came from the Aspics; but if they did, one of 'em went back.

"All I could do was to hustle back to that Boca place and panhandle Major Bing. He detached himself from enough of his winnings to buy me a ticket home. And I'm back again on the job at Chubb's, sir, and I'm going to hold it steady. Come round, and you'll find the steaks as good as ever."

I wondered what Hunky Magee thought about his own story; so I asked him if he had any theories about reincarnation and transmogrification and such mysteries as he had touched upon.

"Nothing like that," said Hunky, positively. "What ailed High Jack was too much booze and education. They'll do an Indian up every time."

"But what about Miss Blue Feather?" I persisted.

"Say," said Hunky, with a grin, "that little lady that stole High Jack certainly did give me a jar when I first took a look at her, but it was only for a minute. You remember I told you High Jack said that Miss Florence Blue Feather disappeared from home about a year ago? Well, where she landed four days later was in as neat a five-room flat on East Twenty-third Street as you ever walked sideways through and she's been Mrs. Magee ever since."

THE MOMENT OF VICTORY

Ben Granger is a war veteran aged twenty-nine, which should enable you to guess the war. He is also principal merchant and postmaster of Cadiz, a little town over which the breezes from the Gulf of Mexico perpetually blow.

Ben helped to hurl the Don from his stronghold in the Greater Antilles; and then, hiking across half the world, he marched as a corporal-usher up and down the blazing tropic aisles of the open-air college in which the Filipino was schooled. Now, with his bayonet beaten into a cheese-slicer, he rallies his corporal's guard of cronies

in the shade of his well-whittled porch, instead of in the matted
jungles of Mindanao. Always have his interest and choice been
for deeds rather than for words; but the consideration and digestion
of motives is not beyond him, as this story, which is his, will attest.

"What is it," he asked me one moonlit eve, as we sat among his boxes
and barrels, "that generally makes men go through dangers, and fire,
and trouble, and starvation, and battle, and such rucouses? What does
a man do it for? Why does he try to outdo his fellow-humans, and be
braver and stronger and more daring and showy than even his best
friends are? What's his game? What does he expect to get out of it?
He don't do it just for the fresh air and exercise. What would you
say, now, Bill, that an ordinary man expects, generally speaking, for
his efforts along the line of ambition and extraordinary hustling in
the marketplaces, forums, shooting-galleries, lyceums, battle-fields,
links, cinder-paths, and arenas of the civilized and vice versa places
of the world?"

"Well, Ben," said I, with judicial seriousness, "I think we might
safely limit the number of motives of a man who seeks fame to three-to
ambition, which is a desire for popular applause; to avarice, which
looks to the material side of success; and to love of some woman whom
he either possesses or desires to possess."

Ben pondered over my words while a mocking-bird on the top of a
mesquite by the porch trilled a dozen bars.

"I reckon," said he, "that your diagnosis about covers the case
according to the rules laid down in the copy-books and historical
readers. But what I had in my mind was the case of Willie Robbins, a
person I used to know. I'll tell you about him before I close up the
store, if you don't mind listening.

"Willie was one of our social set up in San Augustine. I was clerking
there then for Brady & Murchison, wholesale dry-goods and ranch
supplies. Willie and I belonged to the same german club and athletic
association and military company. He played the triangle in our
serenading and quartet crowd that used to ring the welkin three nights
a week somewhere in town.

"Willie jibed with his name considerable. He weighed about as much as
a hundred pounds of veal in his summer suitings, and he had a 'where-
is-Mary?' expression on his features so plain that you could almost
see the wool growing on him.

"And yet you couldn't fence him away from the girls with barbed wire.
You know that kind of young fellows-a kind of a mixture of fools and

angels-they rush in and fear to tread at the same time; but they never fail to tread when they get the chance. He was always on hand when 'a joyful occasion was had,' as the morning paper would say, looking as happy as a king full, and at the same time as uncomfortable as a raw oyster served with sweet pickles. He danced like he had hind hobbles on; and he had a vocabulary of about three hundred and fifty words that he made stretch over four germans a week, and plagiarized from to get him through two ice-cream suppers and a Sunday-night call. He seemed to me to be a sort of a mixture of Maltese kitten, sensitive plant, and a member of a stranded Two Orphans company.

"I'll give you an estimate of his physiological and pictorial make-up, and then I'll stick spurs into the sides of my narrative.

"Willie inclined to the Caucasian in his coloring and manner of style. His hair was opalescent and his conversation fragmentary. His eyes were the same blue shade as the china dog's on the right-hand corner of your Aunt Ellen's mantelpiece. He took things as they come, and I never felt any hostility against him. I let him live, and so did others.

"But what does this Willie do but coax his heart out of his boots and lose it to Myra Allison, the liveliest, brightest, keenest, smartest, and prettiest girl in San Augustine. I tell you, she had the blackest eyes, the shiniest curls, and the most tantalizing - Oh, no, you're off - I wasn't a victim. I might have been, but I knew better. I kept out. Joe Granberry was It from the start. He had everybody else beat a couple of leagues and thence east to a stake and mound. But, anyhow, Myra was a nine-pound, full-merino, fall-clip fleece, sacked and loaded on a four-horse team for San Antone.

"One night there was an ice-cream sociable at Mrs. Colonel Spraggins', in San Augustine. We fellows had a big room up-stairs opened up for us to put our hats and things in, and to comb our hair and put on the clean collars we brought along inside the sweat-bands of our hats-in short, a room to fix up in just like they have everywhere at high-toned doings. A little farther down the hall was the girls' room, which they used to powder up in, and so forth. Downstairs we, that is, the San Augustine Social Cotillion and Merrymakers' Club, had a stretcher put down in the parlor where our dance was going on.

"Willie Robbins and me happened to be up in our cloak-room, I believe we called it when Myra Allison skipped through the hall on her way down-stairs from the girls' room. Willie was standing before the mirror, deeply interested in smoothing down the blond grass-plot on his head, which seemed to give him lots of trouble. Myra was always full of life and devilment. She stopped and stuck her head in our door. She certainly was good-looking. But I knew how Joe Granberry stood with her. So did Willie; but he kept on ba-a-a-ing after her and following her around. He had a system of persistence that didn't coincide with pale hair and light eyes.

"'Hello, Willie!' says Myra. 'What are you doing to yourself in the glass?'

"I'm trying to look fly,' says Willie.

"'Well, you never could be fly,' says Myra, with her special laugh, which was the provokingest sound I ever heard except the rattle of an empty canteen against my saddle-horn.

"I looked around at Willie after Myra had gone. He had a kind of a lily-white look on him which seemed to show that her remark had, as you might say, disrupted his soul. I never noticed anything in what she said that sounded particularly destructive to a man's ideas of self-consciousness; but he was set back to an extent you could scarcely imagine.

"After we went down-stairs with our clean collars on, Willie never went near Myra again that night. After all, he seemed to be a diluted kind of a skim-milk sort of a chap, and I never wondered that Joe Granberry beat him out.

"The next day the battleship Maine was blown up, and then pretty soon somebody-I reckon it was Joe Bailey, or Ben Tillman, or maybe the Government-declared war against Spain.

"Well, everybody south of Mason & Hamlin's line knew that the North by itself couldn't whip a whole country the size of Spain. So the Yankees commenced to holler for help, and the Johnny Rebs answered the call. 'We're coming, Father William, a hundred thousand strong and then some,' was the way they sang it. And the old party lines drawn by Sherman's march and the Kuklux and nine-cent cotton and the Jim Crow street-car ordinances faded away. We became one undivided. country, with no North, very little East, a good-sized chunk of West, and a South that loomed up as big as the first foreign label on a new eight-dollar suit-case.

"Of course the dogs of war weren't a complete pack without a yelp from the San Augustine Rifles, Company D, of the Fourteenth Texas Regiment. Our company was among the first to land in Cuba and strike terror into the hearts of the foe. I'm not going to give you a history of the war, I'm just dragging it in to fill out my story about Willie Robbins, just as the Republican party dragged it in to help out the election in 1898.

"If anybody ever had heroitis, it was that Willie Robbins. From the minute he set foot on the soil of the tyrants of Castile he seemed to engulf danger as a cat laps up cream. He certainly astonished every man in our company, from the captain up. You'd have expected him to gravitate naturally to the job of an orderly to the colonel, or typewriter in the commissary but not any. He created the part of the flaxen-haired boy hero who lives and gets back home with the goods, instead of dying with an important despatch in his hands at his colonel's feet.

"Our company got into a section of Cuban scenery where one of the messiest and most unsung portions of the campaign occurred. We were out every day capering around in the bushes, and having little skirmishes with the Spanish troops that looked more like kind of tired-out feuds than anything else. The war was a joke to us, and of no interest to them. We never could see it any other way than as a howling farce-comedy that the San Augustine Rifles were actually fighting to uphold the Stars and Stripes. And the blamed little senors didn't get enough pay to make them care whether they were patriots or traitors. Now and then somebody would get killed. It seemed like a waste of life to me. I was at Coney Island when I went to New York once, and one of them down-hill skidding apparatuses they call 'roller-coasters' flew the track and killed a man in a brown sack-suit. Whenever the Spaniards shot one of our men, it struck me as just about as unnecessary and regrettable as that was.

"But I'm dropping Willie Robbins out of the conversation.

"He was out for bloodshed, laurels, ambition, medals, recommendations, and all other forms of military glory. And he didn't seem to be afraid of any of the recognized forms of military danger, such as Spaniards, cannon-balls, canned beef, gunpowder, or nepotism. He went forth with his pallid hair and china-blue eyes and ate up Spaniards like you would sardines a la canopy. Wars and rumbles of wars never flustered him. He would stand guard-duty, mosquitoes, hardtack, treat, and fire with equally perfect unanimity. No blondes in history ever come in comparison distance of him except the Jack of Diamonds and Queen Catherine of Russia.

"I remember, one time, a little caballard of Spanish men sauntered out from behind a patch of sugar-cane and shot Bob Turner, the first sergeant of our company, while we were eating dinner. As required by the army regulations, we fellows went through the usual tactics of falling into line, saluting the enemy, and loading and firing, kneeling.

"That wasn't the Texas way of scrapping; but, being a very important addendum and annex to the regular army, the San Augustine Rifles had to conform to the red-tape system of getting even.

"By the time we had got out our 'Upton's Tactics,' turned to page fifty-seven, said 'one – two – three – one – two - three' a couple of times, and got blank cartridges into our Springfields, the Spanish outfit had smiled repeatedly, rolled and lit cigarettes by squads, and walked away contemptuously.

"I went straight to Captain Floyd, and says to him: 'Sam, I don't think this war is a straight game. You know as well as I do that Bob Turner was one of the whitest fellows that ever threw a leg over a saddle, and now these wirepullers in Washington have fixed his clock. He's politically and ostensibly dead. It ain't fair. Why should they keep this thing up? If they want Spain licked, why don't they turn the San Augustine Rifles and Joe Seely's ranger company and a car-load of West Texas deputy-sheriffs onto these Spaniards, and let us exonerate them from the face of the earth? I never did,' says I, 'care much about fighting by the Lord Chesterfield ring rules. I'm going to hand in my resignation and go home if anybody else I am personally acquainted with gets hurt in this war. If you can get somebody in my place, Sam,' says I, 'I'll quit the first of next week. I don't want to work in an army that don't give its help a chance. Never mind my wages,' says I; 'let the Secretary of the Treasury keep 'em.'

"'Well, Ben,' says the captain to me, 'your allegations and estimations of the tactics of war, government, patriotism, guard-mounting, and democracy are all right. But I've looked into the system of international arbitration and the ethics of justifiable slaughter a little closer, maybe, than you have. Now, you can hand in your resignation the first of next week if you are so minded. But if you do,' says Sam, 'I'll order a corporal's guard to take you over by that limestone bluff on the creek and shoot enough lead into you to ballast a submarine air-ship. I'm captain of this company, and I've swore allegiance to the Amalgamated States regardless of sectional, secessional, and Congressional differences. Have you got any smoking-tobacco?' winds up Sam. 'Mine got wet when I swum the creek this morning.'

"The reason I drag all this non ex parte evidence in is because Willie Robbins was standing there listening to us. I was a second sergeant and he was a private then, but among us Texans and Westerners there never was as much tactics and subordination as there was in the regular army. We never called our captain anything but 'Sam' except when there was a lot of major-generals and admirals around, so as to preserve the discipline.

"And says Willie Robbins to me, in a sharp construction of voice much unbecoming to his light hair and previous record:

"'You ought to be shot, Ben, for emitting any such sentiments. A man that won't fight for his country is worse than a, horse-thief. If I was the cap, I'd put you in the guard-house for thirty days on round steak and tamales. War,' says Willie, 'is great and glorious. I didn't know you were a coward.'

"'I'm not,' says I. 'If I was, I'd knock some of the pallidness off of your marble brow. I'm lenient with you,' I says, 'just as I am with the Spaniards, because you have always reminded me of something with mushrooms on the side. Why, you little Lady of Shalott,' says I, 'you underdone leader of cotillions, you glassy fashion and moulded form, you white-pine soldier made in the Cisalpine Alps in Germany for the late New-Year trade, do you know of whom you are talking to? We've been in the same social circle,' says I, 'and I've put up with you because you seemed so meek and self-un-satisfying. I don't understand why you have so sudden taken a personal interest in chivalrousness and murder. Your nature's undergone a complete revelation. Now, how is it?'

"'Well, you wouldn't understand, Ben,' says Willie, giving one of his refined smiles and turning away.

"'Come back here!' says I, catching him by the tail of his khaki coat. 'You've made me kind of mad, in spite of the aloofness in which I have heretofore held you. You are out for making a success in this hero business, and I believe I know what for. You are doing it either because you are crazy or because you expect to catch some girl by it. Now, if it's a girl, I've got something here to show you.'

"I wouldn't have done it, but I was plumb mad. I pulled a San Augustine paper out of my hip-pocket, and showed him an item. It was a half a column about the marriage of Myra Allison and Joe Granberry.

"Willie laughed, and I saw I hadn't touched him.

"'Oh,' says he, 'everybody knew that was going to happen. I heard about that a week ago.' And then he gave me the laugh again.

"'All right,' says I. 'Then why do you so recklessly chase the bright rainbow of fame? Do you expect to be elected President, or do you belong to a suicide club ?'

"And then Captain Sam interferes.

"'You gentlemen quit jawing and go back to your quarters,' says he, 'or I'll have you escorted to the guard-house. Now, scat, both of you! Before you go, which one of you has got any chewing-tobacco?'

"'We're off, Sam,' says I. 'It's supper-time, anyhow. But what do you think of what we was talking about? I've noticed you throwing out a good many grappling-hooks for this here balloon called fame. What's ambition, anyhow? What does a man risk his life day after day for? Do you know of anything he gets in the end that can pay him for the trouble? I want to go back home,' says I. 'I don't care whether Cuba sinks or swims, and I don't give a pipeful of rabbit tobacco whether Queen Sophia Christina or Charlie Culberson rules these fairy isles; and I don't want my name on any list except the list of survivors. But I've noticed you, Sam,' says I, 'seeking the bubble notoriety in the cannon's larynx a number of times. Now, what do you do it for? Is it ambition, business, or some freckle-faced Pheebe at home that you are heroing for ?'

"'Well, Ben,' says Sam, kind of hefting his sword out from between his knees, 'as your superior officer I could court-martial you for attempted cowardice and desertion. But I won't. And I'll tell you why I'm trying for promotion and the usual honors of war and conquest. A major gets more pay than a captain, and I need the money.'

"'Correct for you!' says I. 'I can understand that. Your system of fame-seeking is rooted in the deepest soil of patriotism. But I can't comprehend,' says I, 'why Willie Robbins, whose folks at home are well off, and who used to be as meek and undesirous of notice as a cat with cream on his whiskers, should all at once develop into a warrior bold with the most fire-eating kind of proclivities. And the girl in his case seems to have been eliminated by marriage to another fellow. I reckon,' says I, 'it's a plain case of just common ambition. He wants his name, maybe, to go thundering down the coroners of time. It must be that.'

"Well, without itemizing his deeds, Willie sure made good as a hero. He simply spent most of his time on his knees begging our captain to send him on forlorn hopes and dangerous scouting expeditions. In every fight he was the first man to mix it at close quarters with the Don Alfonsos. He got three or four bullets planted in various parts of his autonomy. Once he went off with a detail of eight men and captured a whole company of Spanish. He kept Captain Floyd busy writing out recommendations of his bravery to send in to head-quarters; and he began to accumulate medals for all kinds of things-heroism and target-shooting and valor and tactics and uninsubordination, and all the little accomplishments that look good to the third assistant secretaries of the War Department.

"Finally, Cap Floyd got promoted to be a major-general, or a knight commander of the main herd, or something like that. He pounded around on a white horse, all desecrated up with gold-leaf and hen-feathers and a Good Templar's hat, and wasn't allowed by the regulations to speak to us. And Willie Robbins was made captain of our company.

"And maybe he didn't go after the wreath of fame then! As far as I could see it was him that ended the war. He got eighteen of us boys, friends of his, too, killed in battles that he stirred up himself, and that didn't seem to me necessary at all. One night he took twelve of us and waded through a little nil about a hundred and ninety yards wide, and climbed a couple of mountains, and sneaked through a mile of neglected shrubbery and a couple of rock-quarries and into a rye-straw village, and captured a Spanish general named, as they said, Benny Veedus. Benny seemed to me hardly worth the trouble, being a blackish man without shoes or cuffs, and anxious to surrender and throw himself on the commissary of his foe.

"But that job gave Willie the big boost he wanted. The San Augustine News and the Galveston, St. Louis, New York, and Kansas City papers printed his picture and columns of stuff about him. Old San Augustine simply went crazy over its 'gallant son.' The News had an editorial tearfully begging the Government to call off the regular army and the national guard, and let Willie carry on the rest of the war single-handed. It said that a refusal to do so would be regarded as a proof that the Northern jealousy of the South was still as rampant as ever.

"If the war hadn't ended pretty soon, I don't know to what heights of gold braid and encomiums Willie would have climbed; but it did. There was a secession of hostilities just three days after he was appointed a colonel, and got in three more medals by registered mail, and shot two Spaniards while they were drinking lemonade in an ambuscade.

"Our company went back to San Augustine when the war was over. There wasn't anywhere else for it to go. And what do you think? The old town notified us in print, by wire cable, special delivery, and a nigger named Saul sent on a gray mule to San Antone, that they was going to give us the biggest blow-out, complimentary, alimentary, and elementary, that ever disturbed the kildees on the sand-flats outside of the immediate contiguity of the city.

"I say 'we,' but it was all meant for ex-Private, Captain de facto, and Colonel-elect Willie Robbins. The town was crazy about him. They notified us that the reception they were going to put up would make the Mardi Gras in New Orleans look like an afternoon tea in Bury St. Edmunds with a curate's aunt.

"Well, the San Augustine Rifles got back home on schedule time. Everybody was at the depot giving forth Roosevelt-Democrat - they used to be called Rebel - yells. There was two brass-bands, and the mayor, and schoolgirls in white frightening the street-car horses by throwing Cherokee roses in the streets, and-well, maybe you've seen a celebration by a town that was inland and out of water.

"They wanted Brevet-Colonel Willie to get into a carriage and be drawn by prominent citizens and some of the city aldermen to the armory, but he stuck to his company and marched at the head of it up Sam Houston Avenue. The buildings on both sides was covered with flags and audiences, and everybody hollered 'Robbins!' or 'Hello, Willie!' as we marched up in files of fours. I never saw a illustriouser-looking human in my life than Willie was. He had at least seven or eight medals and diplomas and decorations on the breast of his khaki coat; he was sunburnt the color of a saddle, and he certainly done himself proud.

"They told us at the depot that the courthouse was to be illuminated at half-past seven, and there would be speeches and chili-con-came at the Palace Hotel. Miss Delphine Thompson was to read an original poem by James Whitcomb Ryan, and Constable Hooker had promised us a salute of nine guns from Chicago that he had arrested that day.

"After we had disbanded in the armory, Willie says to me:

"'Want to walk out a piece with me?'

"'Why, yes,' says I, 'if it ain't so far that we can't hear the tumult and the shouting die away. I'm hungry myself,' says I, 'and I'm pining for some home grub, but I'll go with you.'

"Willie steered me down some side streets till we came to a little white cottage in a new lot with a twenty-by-thirty-foot lawn decorated with brickbats and old barrel-staves.

"'Halt and give the countersign,' says I to Willie. 'Don't you know this dugout? It's the bird's-nest that Joe Granberry built before he married Myra Allison. What you going there for?'

"But Willie already had the gate open. He walked up the brick walk to the steps, and I went with him. Myra was sitting in a rocking-chair on the porch, sewing. Her hair was smoothed back kind of hasty and tied in a knot. I never noticed till then that she had freckles. Joe was at one side of the porch, in his shirtsleeves, with no collar on, and no signs of a shave, trying to scrape out a hole among the brickbats and tin cans to plant a little fruit-tree in. He looked up but never said a word, and neither did Myra.

"Willie was sure dandy-looking in his uniform, with medals strung on his breast and his new gold-handled sword. You'd never have taken him for the little white-headed snipe that the girls used to order about and make fun of. He just stood there for a minute, looking at Myra with a peculiar little smile on his face; and then he says to her, slow, and kind of holding on to his words with his teeth:

"'Oh, I don't know! Maybe I could if I tried!'

"That was all that was said. Willie raised his hat, and we walked away.

"And, somehow, when he said that, I remembered, all of a sudden, the night of that dance and Willie brushing his hair before the looking-glass, and Myra sticking her head in the door to guy him.

"When we got back to Sam Houston Avenue, Willie says:

"'Well, so long, Ben. I'm going down home and get off my shoes and take a rest.'

"'You?' says I. 'What's the matter with you? Ain't the court-house jammed with everybody in town waiting to honor the hero? And two brass-bands, and recitations and flags and jags and grub to follow waiting for you?'

"Willie sighs.

"'All right, Ben,' says he. 'Darned if I didn't forget all about that.'

"And that's why I say," concluded Ben Granger, "that you can't tell where ambition begins any more than you can where it is going to wind up."

THE HEAD-HUNTER

When the war between Spain and George Dewey was over, I went to the Philippine Islands. There I remained as bushwhacker correspondent for my paper until its managing editor notified me that an eight-hundred-word cablegram describing the grief of a pet carabao over the death of an infant Moro was not considered by the office to be war news. So I resigned, and came home.

On board the trading-vessel that brought me back I pondered much upon the strange things I had sensed in the weird archipelago of the yellow-brown people. The manoeuvres and skirmishings of the petty war interested me not: I was spellbound by the outlandish and unreadable countenance of that race that had turned its expressionless gaze upon us out of an unguessable past.

Particularly during my stay in Mindanao had I been fascinated and attracted by that delightfully original tribe of heathen known as the head-hunters. Those grim, flinty, relentless little men, never seen, but chilling the warmest noonday by the subtle terror of their concealed presence, paralleling the trail of their prey through unmapped forests, across perilous mountain-tops, adown bottomless chasms, into uninhabitable jungles, always near with the invisible hand of death uplifted, betraying their pursuit only by such signs as a beast or a bird or a gliding serpent might make-a twig crackling in the awful, sweat-soaked night, a drench of dew showering from the screening foliage of a giant tree, a whisper at even from the rushes of a water-level-a hint of death for every mile and every hour-they amused me greatly, those little fellows of one idea.

When you think of it, their method is beautifully and almost hilariously effective and simple.

You have your hut in which you live and carry out the destiny that was decreed for you. Spiked to the jamb of your bamboo doorway is a basket made of green withes, plaited. From time to time, as vanity or ennui or love or jealousy or ambition may move you, you creep forth with your snickersnee and take up the silent trail. Back from it you come, triumphant, bearing the severed, gory head of your victim, which you deposit with pardonable pride in the basket at the side of your door. It may be the head of your enemy, your friend, or a stranger, according as competition, jealousy, or simple sportiveness has been your incentive to labor.

In any case, your reward is certain. The village men, in passing, stop to congratulate you, as your neighbor on weaker planes of life stops to admire and praise the begonias in your front yard. Your particular brown maid lingers, with fluttering bosom, casting soft tiger's eyes at the evidence of your love for her. You chew betel-nut and listen, content, to the intermittent soft drip from the ends of the severed neck arteries. And you show your teeth and grunt like a water-buffalo, which is as near as you can come to laughing-at the thought that the cold, acephalous body of your door ornament is being spotted by wheeling vultures in the Mindanaoan wilds.

Truly, the life of the merry head-hunter captivated me. He had reduced art and philosophy to a simple code. To take your adversary's head, to basket it at the portal of your castle, to see it lying there, a dead thing, with its cunning and stratagems and power gone. Is there a better way to foil his plots, to refute his arguments, to establish your superiority over his skill and wisdom?

The ship that brought me home was captained by an erratic Swede, who changed his course and deposited me, with genuine compassion, in a small town on the Pacific coast of one of the Central American republics, a few hundred miles south of the port to which he had engaged to convey me. But I was wearied of movement and exotic fancies; so I leaped contentedly upon the firm sands of the village of Mojada, telling myself I should be sure to find there the rest that I craved. After all, far better to linger there (I thought), lulled by the sedative plash of the waves and the rustling of palm-fronds, than to sit upon the horsehair sofa of my parental home in the East, and there, cast down by currant wine and cake, and scourged by fatuous relatives, drivel into the ears of gaping neighbors sad stories of the death of colonial governors.

When I first saw Chloe Greene she was standing, all in white, in the doorway of her father's tile-roofed 'dobe house. She was polishing a silver cup with a cloth, and she looked like a pearl laid against black velvet. She turned on me a flatteringly protracted but a wiltingly disapproving gaze, and then went inside, humming a light song to indicate the value she placed upon my existence.

Small wonder: for Dr. Stamford (the most disreputable professional man between Juneau and Valparaiso) and I were zigzagging along the turfy street, tunelessly singing the words of Auld Lang Syne to the air of Muzzer's Little Coal-Black Coon. We had come from the ice factory, which was Mojada's palace of wickedness, where we had been playing billiards and opening black bottles, white with frost, that we dragged with strings out of old Sandoval's ice-cold vats.

I turned in sudden rage to Dr. Stamford, as sober as the verger of a cathedral. In a moment I had become aware that we were swine cast before a pearl.

"You beast," I said, "this is half your doing. And the other half is the fault of this cursed country. I'd better have gone back to Sleepy-town and died in a wild orgy of currant wine and buns than to have had this happen."

Stamford filled the empty street with his roaring laughter.

"You too!" he cried. "And all as quick as the popping of a cork.

Well, she does seem to strike agreeably upon the retina. But don't burn your fingers. All Mojada will tell you that Louis Devoe is the man.

"We will see about that," said I. "And, perhaps, whether he is a man as well as the man."

I lost no time in meeting Louis Devoe. That was easily accomplished, for the foreign colony in Mojada numbered scarce a dozen; and they gathered daily at a half-decent hotel kept by a Turk, where they managed to patch together the fluttering rags of country and civilization that were left them. I sought Devoe before I did my pearl of the doorway, because I had learned a little of the game of war, and knew better than to strike for a prize before testing the strength of the enemy.

A sort of cold dismay-something akin to fear-filled me when I had estimated him. I found a man so perfectly poised, so charming, so deeply learned in the world's rituals, so full of tact, courtesy, and hospitality, so endowed with grace and ease and a kind of careless, haughty power that I almost overstepped the bounds in probing him, in turning him on the spit to find the weak point that I so craved for him to have. But I left him whole-I had to make bitter acknowledgment to myself that Louis Devoe was a gentleman worthy of my best blows; and I swore to give him them. He was a great merchant of the country, a wealthy importer and exporter. All day he sat in a fastidiously appointed office, surrounded by works of art and evidences of his high culture, directing through glass doors and windows the affairs of his house.

In person he was slender and hardly tall. His small, well-shaped head was covered with thick, brown hair, trimmed short, and he wore a thick, brown beard also cut close and to a fine point. His manners were a pattern.

Before long I had become a regular and a welcome visitor at the Greene home. I shook my wild habits from me like a worn-out cloak. I trained for the conflict with the care of a prize-fighter and the self-denial of a Brahmin.

As for Chloe Greene, I shall weary you with no sonnets to her eyebrow. She was a splendidly feminine girl, as wholesome as a November pippin, and no more mysterious than a windowpane. She had whimsical little theories that she had deduced from life, and that fitted the maxims of Epictetus like princess gowns. I wonder, after all, if that old duffer wasn't rather wise!

Chloe had a father, the Reverend Homer Greene, and an intermittent mother, who sometimes palely presided over a twilight teapot. The Reverend Homer was a burr-like man with a life-work. He was writing a concordance to the Scriptures, and had arrived as far as Kings. Being, presumably, a suitor for his daughter's hand, I was timber for his literary outpourings. I had the family tree of Israel drilled into my head until I used to cry aloud in my sleep: "And Aminadab begat Jay Eye See," and so forth, until he had tackled another book. I once made a calculation that the Reverend Homer's concordance would be worked up as far as the Seven Vials mentioned in Revelations about the third day after they were opened.

Louis Devoe, as well as I, was a visitor and an intimate friend of the Greenes. It was there I met him the oftenest, and a more agreeable' man or a more accomplished I have never hated in my life.

Luckily or unfortunately, I came to be accepted as a Boy. My appearance was youthful, and I suppose I had that pleading and homeless air that always draws the motherliness that is in women and the cursed theories and hobbies of pater-familiases.

Chloe called me "Tommy," and made sisterly fun of my attempts to woo her. With Devoe she was vastly more reserved. He was the man of romance, one to stir her imagination and deepest feelings had her fancy leaned toward him. I was closer to her, but standing in no glamour; I had the task before me of winning her in what seems to me the American way of fighting with cleanness and pluck and everyday devotion to break away the barriers of friendship that divided us, and to take her, if I could, between sunrise and dark, abetted by neither moonlight nor music nor foreign wiles.

Chloe gave no sign of bestowing her blithe affections upon either of us. But one day she let out to me an inkling of what she preferred in a man. It was tremendously interesting to me, but not illuminating as to its application. I had been tormenting her for the dozenth time with the statement and catalogue of my sentiments toward her.

"Tommy," said she, "I don't want a man to show his love for me by leading an army against another country and blowing people off the earth with cannons."

"If you mean that the opposite way," I answered, "as they say women do, I'll see what I can do. The papers are full of this diplomatic row in Russia. My people know some big people in Washington who are right next to the army people, and I could get an artillery commission and -"

"I'm not that way," interrupted Chloe. "I mean what I say. It isn't the big things that are done in the world, Tommy, that count with a woman. When the knights were riding abroad in their armor to slay dragons, many a stay-at-home page won a lonesome lady's hand by being on the spot to pick up her glove and be quick with her cloak when the wind blew. The man I am to like best, whoever he shall be, must show his love in little ways. He must never forget, after hearing it once, that I do not like to have any one walk at my left side; that I detest bright-colored neckties; that I prefer to sit with my back to a light; that I like candied violets; that I must not be talked to when I am looking at the moonlight shining on water, and that I very, very often long for dates stuffed with English walnuts."

"Frivolity," I said, with a frown. "Any well-trained servant would be equal to such details."

"And he must remember," went on Chloe, to remind me of what I want when I do not know, myself, what I want."

"You're rising in the scale," I said. "What you seem to need is a first-class clairvoyant."

"And if I say that I am dying to hear a Beethoven sonata, and stamp my foot when I say it, he must know by that that what my soul craves is salted almonds; and he will have them ready in his pocket."

"Now," said I, "I am at a loss. I do not know whether your soul's affinity is to be an impresario or a fancy grocer."

Chole turned her pearly smile upon me.

"Take less than half of what I said as a jest," she went on. "And don't think too lightly of the little things, Boy. Be a paladin if you must, but don't let it show on you. Most women are only very big children, and most men are only very little ones. Please us; don't try to overpower us. When we want a hero we can make one out of even a plain grocer the third time he catches our handkerchief before it falls to the ground."

That evening I was taken down with pernicious fever. That is a kind of coast fever with improvements and high-geared attachments. Your temperature goes up among the threes and fours and remains there, laughing scornfully and feverishly at the cinchona trees and the coal-tar derivatives. Pernicious fever is a case for a simple mathematician instead of a doctor. It is merely this formula: Vitality + the desire to live = the duration of the fever the result.

I took to my bed in the two-roomed thatched hut where I had been comfortably established, and sent for a gallon of rum. That was not for myself. Drunk, Stamford was the best doctor between the Andes and the Pacific. He came, sat at my bedside, and drank himself into condition.

"My boy," said he, "my lily-white and reformed Romeo, medicine will do you no good. But I will give you quinine, which, being bitter, will arouse in you hatred and anger-two stimulants that will add ten per cent. to your chances. You are as strong as a caribou calf, and you will get well if the fever doesn't get in a knockout blow when you're off your guard."

For two weeks I lay on my back feeling like a Hindoo widow on a burning ghat. Old Atasca, an untrained Indian nurse, sat near the door like a petrified statue of What's-the-Use, attending to her duties, which were, mainly, to see that time went by without slipping a cog. Sometimes I would fancy myself back in the Philippines, or, at worse times, sliding off the horsehair sofa in Sleepytown.

One afternoon I ordered Atasca to vamose, and got up and dressed carefully. I took my temperature, which I was pleased to find 104. I paid almost dainty attention to my dress, choosing solicitously a necktie of a dull and subdued hue. The mirror showed that I was looking little the worse from my illness. The fever gave brightness to my eyes and color to my face. And while I looked at my reflection my color went and came again as I thought of Chloe Greene and the millions of eons that had passed since I'd seen her, and of Louis Devoe and the time he had gained on me.

I went straight to her house. I seemed to float rather than walk; I hardly felt the ground under my feet; I thought pernicious fever must be a great boon to make one feel so strong.

I found Chloe and Louis Devoe sitting under the awning in front of the house. She jumped up and met me with a double handshake.

"I'm glad, glad, glad to see you out again!" she cried, every word a pearl strung on the string of her sentence. "You are well, Tommy or better, of course. I wanted to come to see you, but they wouldn't let me.

"Oh yes," said I, carelessly, "it was nothing. Merely a little fever. I am out again, as you see."

We three sat there and talked for half an hour or so. Then Chloe looked out yearningly and almost piteously across the ocean. I could see in her sea-blue eyes some deep and intense desire. Devoe, curse him! saw it too.

"What is it?" we asked, in unison.

"Cocoanut-pudding," said Chloe, pathetically. "I've wanted some, oh, so badly, for two days. It's got beyond a wish; it's an obsession.

"The cocoanut season is over," said Devoe, in that voice of his that gave thrilling interest to his most commonplace words. "I hardly think one could be found in Mojada. The natives never use them except when they are green and the milk is fresh. They sell all the ripe ones to the fruiterers."

"Wouldn't a broiled lobster or a Welsh rabbit do as well?" I remarked, with the engaging idiocy of a pernicious-fever convalescent.

Chloe came as near to pouting as a sweet disposition and a perfect profile would allow her to come.

The Reverend Homer poked his ermine-lined face through the doorway and added a concordance to the conversation.

"Sometimes," said he, "old Campos keeps the dried nuts in his little store on the hill. But it would be far better, my daughter, to restrain unusual desires, and partake thankfully of the daily dishes that the Lord has set before us."

"Stuff!" said I.

"How was that?" asked the Reverend Homer, sharply.

"I say it's tough," said I, "to drop into the vernacular, that Miss Greene should be deprived of the food she desires-a simple thing like kalsomine-pudding. Perhaps," I continued, solicitously, "some pickled walnuts or a fricassee of Hungarian butternuts would do as well."

Every one looked at me with a slight exhibition of curiosity.

Louis Devoe arose and made his adieus. I watched him until he had sauntered slowly and grandiosely to the corner, around which he turned to reach his great warehouse and store. Chloe made her excuses, and went inside for a few minutes to attend to some detail affecting the seven-o'clock dinner. She was a passed mistress in housekeeping. I had tasted her puddings and bread with beatitude.

When all had gone, I turned casually and saw a basket made of plaited

green withes hanging by a nail outside the door-jamb. With a rush
that made my hot temples throb there came vividly to my mind
recollections of the head-hunters, those grim, flinty, relentless
little men, never seen, but chilling the warmest noonday by the subtle
terror of their concealed presence. . . . From time to time, as
vanity or ennui or love or jealousy or ambition may move him, one
creeps forth with his snickersnee and takes up the silent trail. . .
. Back he comes, triumphant, bearing the severed, gory head of his
victim . . . His particular brown or white maid lingers, with
fluttering bosom, casting soft tiger's eyes at the evidence of his
love for her.

I stole softly from the house and returned to my hut. From its
supporting nails in the wall I took a machete as heavy as a butcher's
cleaver and sharper than a safety-razor. And then I chuckled softly
to myself, and set out to the fastidiously appointed private office of
Monsieur Louis Devoe, usurper to the hand of the Pearl of the Pacific.

He was never slow at thinking; he gave one look at my face and another
at the weapon in my hand as I entered his door, and then he seemed to
fade from my sight. I ran to the back door, kicked it open, and saw
him running like a deer up the road toward the wood that began two
hundred yards away. I was after him, with a shout. I remember
hearing children and women screaming, and seeing them flying from the
road.

He was fleet, but I was stronger. A mile, and I had almost come up
with him. He doubled cunningly and dashed into a brake that extended
into a small canon. I crashed through this after him, and in five
minutes had him cornered in an angle of insurmountable cliffs. There
his instinct of self-preservation steadied him, as it will steady even
animals at bay. He turned to me, quite calm, with a ghastly smile.

"Oh, Rayburn!" he said, with such an awful effort at ease that I was
impolite enough to laugh rudely in his face. "Oh, Rayburn!" said he,
"come, let's have done with this nonsense. Of course, I know it's the
fever and you're not yourself; but collect yourself, man-give me that
ridiculous weapon, now, and let's go back and talk it over."

"I will go back," said I, "carrying your head with me. We will see
how charmingly it can discourse when it lies in the basket at her
door."

"Come," said he, persuasively, "I think better of you than to suppose
that you try this sort of thing as a joke. But even the vagaries of a
fever-crazed lunatic come sometime to a limit. What is this talk
about heads and baskets? Get yourself together and throw away that

absurd cane-chopper. What would Miss Greene think of you?" he ended, with the silky cajolery that one would use toward a fretful child.

"Listen," said I. "At last you have struck upon the right note. What would she think of me? Listen," I repeated.

"There are women," I said, "who look upon horsehair sofas and currant wine as dross. To them even the calculated modulation of your well-trimmed talk sounds like the dropping of rotten plums from a tree in the night. They are the maidens who walk back and forth in the villages, scorning the emptiness of the baskets at the doors of the young men who would win them.

One such as they," I said, "is waiting. Only a fool would try to win a woman by drooling like a braggart in her doorway or by waiting upon her whims like a footman. They are all daughters of Herodias, and to gain their hearts one must lay the heads of his enemies before them with his own hands. Now, bend your neck, Louis Devoe. Do not be a coward as well as a chatterer at a lady's tea-table."

"There, there!" said Devoe, falteringly. "You know me, don't you, Rayburn?"

"Oh yes," I said, "I know you. I know you. I know you. But the basket is empty. The old men of the village and the young men, and both the dark maidens and the ones who are as fair as pearls walk back and forth and see its emptiness. Will you kneel now, or must we have a scuffle? It is not like you to make things go roughly and with bad form. But the basket is waiting for your head."

With that he went to pieces. I had to catch him as he tried to scamper past me like a scared rabbit. I stretched him out and got a foot on his chest, but he squirmed like a worm, although I appealed repeatedly to his sense of propriety and the duty he owed to himself as a gentleman not to make a row.

But at last he gave me the chance, and I swung the machete.

It was not hard work. He flopped like a chicken during the six or seven blows that it took to sever his head; but finally he lay still, and I tied his head in my handkerchief. The eyes opened and shut thrice while I walked a hundred yards. I was red to my feet with the drip, but what did that matter? With delight I felt under my hands the crisp touch of his short, thick, brown hair and close-trimmed beard.

I reached the house of the Greenes and dumped the head of Louis Devoe

into the basket that still hung by the nail in the door-jamb. I sat
in a chair under the awning and waited. The sun was within two hours
of setting. Chloe came out and looked surprised.

"Where have you been, Tommy?" she asked. "You were gone when I
came out."

"Look in the basket," I said, rising to my feet. She looked, and gave
a little scream of delight, I was pleased to note.

"Oh, Tommy!" she said. "It was just what I wanted you to do. It's
leaking a little, but that doesn't matter. Wasn't I telling you? It's the
little things that count. And you remembered."

Little things! She held the ensanguined head of Louis Devoe in her
white apron. Tiny streams of red widened on her apron and dripped
upon the floor. Her face was bright and tender.

"Little things, indeed!" I thought again. "The head-hunters are
right. These are the things that women like you to do for them."

Chloe came close to me. There was no one in sight. She looked tip at
me with sea-blue eyes that said things they had never said before.

"You think of me," she said. "You are the man I was describing. You
think of the little things, and they are what make the world worth
living in. The man for me must consider my little wishes, and make me
happy in small ways. He must bring me little red peaches in December
if I wish for them, and then I will love him till June. I will have
no knight in armor slaying his rival or killing dragons for me. You
please me very well, Tommy."

I stooped and kissed her. Then a moisture broke out on my forehead,
and I began to feel weak. I saw the red stains vanish from Chloe's
apron, and the head of Louis Devoe turn to a brown, dried cocoanut.

"There will be cocoanut-pudding for dinner, Tommy, boy," said Chloe,
gayly, "and you must come. I must go in for a little while."

She vanished in a delightful flutter.

Dr. Stamford tramped up hurriedly. He seized my pulse as though it
were his own property that I had escaped with.

"You are the biggest fool outside of any asylum!" he said, angrily.
"Why did you leave your bed? And the idiotic things you've been
doing! and no wonder, with your pulse going like a sledge-hammer."

"Name some of them," said I.

"Devoe sent for me," said Stamford. "He saw you from his window go to old Campos' store, chase him up the hill with his own yardstick, and then come back and make off with his biggest cocoanut."

"It's the little things that count, after all," said I.

"It's your little bed that counts with you just now," said the doctor. "You come with me at once, or I'll throw up the case. 'You're as loony as a loon."

So I got no cocoanut-pudding that evening, but I conceived a distrust as to the value of the method of the head-hunters. Perhaps for many centuries the maidens of the villages may have been looking wistfully at the heads in the baskets at the doorways, longing for other and lesser trophies.

NO STORY
To avoid having this book hurled into corner of the room by the suspicious reader, I will assert in time that this is not a newspaper story. You will encounter no shirt-sleeved, omniscient city editor, no prodigy "cub" reporter just off the farm, no scoop, no story, no anything.

But if you will concede me the setting of the first scene in the reporters' room of the Morning Beacon, I will repay the favor by keeping strictly my promises set forth above.

I was doing space-work on the Beacon, hoping to be put on a salary. Someone had cleared with a rake or a shovel a small space for me at the end of a long table piled high with exchanges, Congressional Records, and old files. There I did my work. I wrote whatever the city whispered or roared or chuckled to me on my diligent wanderings about its streets. My income was not regular.

One day Tripp came in and leaned on my table. Tripp was something in the mechanical department, I think he had something to do with the pictures, for he smelled of photographers' supplies, and his hands were always stained and cut up with acids. He was about twenty-five and looked forty. Half of his face was covered with short, curly red

whiskers that looked like a door-mat with the "welcome" left off. He was pale and unhealthy and miserable and fawning, and an assiduous borrower of sums ranging from twenty-five cents to a dollar. One dollar was his limit. He knew the extent of his credit as well as the Chemical National Bank knows the amount of H20 that collateral will show on analysis. When he sat on my table he held one hand with the other to keep both from shaking. Whiskey. He had a spurious air of lightness and bravado about him that deceived no one, but was useful in his borrowing because it was so pitifully and perceptibly assumed.

This day I had coaxed from the cashier five shining silver dollars as a grumbling advance on a story that the Sunday editor had reluctantly accepted. So if I was not feeling at peace with the world, at least an armistice had been declared; and I was beginning with ardor to write a description of the Brooklyn Bridge by moonlight.

"Well, Tripp," said I, looking up at him rather impatiently, "how goes it?" He was looking to-day more miserable, more cringing and haggard and downtrodden than I had ever seen him. He was at that stage of misery where he drew your pity so fully that you longed to kick him.

"Have you got a dollar?" asked Tripp, with his most fawning look and his dog-like eyes that blinked in the narrow space between his high-growing matted beard and his low-growing matted hair.

"I have," said I; and again I said, "I have," more loudly and inhospitably, "and four besides. And I had hard work corkscrewing them out of old Atkinson, I can tell you. And I drew them," I continued, "to meet a want - a hiatus - a demand - a need - an exigency –a requirement of exactly five dollars."

I was driven to emphasis by the premonition that I was to lose one of the dollars on the spot.

"I don't want to borrow any," said Tripp, and I breathed again. "I thought you'd like to get put onto a good story," he went on. "I've got a rattling fine one for you. You ought to make it run a column at least. It'll make a dandy if you work it up right. It'll probably cost you a dollar or two to get the stuff. I don't want anything out of it myself."

I became placated. The proposition showed that Tripp appreciated past favors, although he did not return them. If he had been wise enough to strike me for a quarter then he would have got it.

"What is the story ?" I asked, poising my pencil with a finely calculated editorial air.

"I'll tell you," said Tripp. "It's a girl. A beauty. One of the howlingest Amsden's Junes you ever saw. Rosebuds covered with dew-violets in their mossy bed and truck like that. She's lived on Long Island twenty years and never saw New York City before. I ran against her on Thirty-fourth Street. She'd just got in on the East River ferry. I tell you, she's a beauty that would take the hydrogen out of all the peroxides in the world. She stopped me on the street and asked me where she could find George Brown. Asked me where she could find George Brown in New York City! What do you think of that?

"I talked to her, and found that she was going to marry a young farmer named Dodd, Hiram Dodd, next week. But it seems that George Brown still holds the championship in her youthful fancy. George had greased his cowhide boots some years ago, and came to the city to make his fortune. But he forgot to remember to show up again at Greenburg, and Hiram got in as second-best choice. But when it comes to the scratch Ada, her name's Ada Lowery, saddles a nag and rides eight miles to the railroad station and catches the 6.45 A.M. train for the city. Looking for George, you know, you understand about women, George wasn't there, so she wanted him.

"Well, you know, I couldn't leave her loose in Wolftown-on-the-Hudson. I suppose she thought the first person she inquired of would say: 'George Brown ? why, yes, lemme see, he's a short man with light-blue eyes, ain't he? Oh yes, you'll find George on One Hundred and Twenty-fifth Street, right next to the grocery. He's bill-clerk in a saddle-and-harness store.' That's about how innocent and beautiful she is. You know those little Long Island water-front villages like Greenburg--a couple of duck-farms for sport, and clams and about nine summer visitors for industries. That's the kind of a place she comes from. But, say, you ought to see her!

"What could I do? I don't know what money looks like in the morning. And she'd paid her last cent of pocket-money for her railroad ticket except a quarter, which she had squandered on gum-drops. She was eating them out of a paper bag. I took her to a boarding-house on Thirty-second Street where I used to live, and hocked her. She's in soak for a dollar. That's old Mother McGinnis' price per day. I'll show you the house."

"What words are these, Tripp?" said I. "I thought you said you had a story. Every ferryboat that crosses the East River brings or takes away girls from Long Island."

The premature lines on Tripp's face grew deeper. He frowned seriously from his tangle of hair. He separated his hands and emphasized his answer with one shaking forefinger.

"Can't you see," he said, "what a rattling fine story it would make?

You could do it fine. All about the romance, you know, and describe the girl, and put a lot of stuff in it about true love, and sling in a few stickfuls of funny business, joshing the Long Islanders about being green, and, well, you know how to do it. You ought to get fifteen dollars out of it, anyhow. And it'll. cost you only about four dollars. You'll make a clear profit of eleven."

"How will it cost me four dollars?" I asked, suspiciously.

"One dollar to Mrs. McGinnis," Tripp answered, promptly, "and two dollars to pay the girl's fare back home."

"And the fourth dimension?" I inquired, making a rapid mental calculation.

"One dollar to me," said Tripp. "For whiskey. Are you on?"

I smiled enigmatically and spread my elbows as if to begin writing again. But this grim, abject, specious, subservient, burr-like wreck of a man would not be shaken off. His forehead suddenly became shiningly moist.

"Don't you see," he said, with a sort of desperate calmness, "that this girl has got to be sent home to-day, not to-night nor to-morrow, but to-day? I can't do anything for her. You know, I'm the janitor and corresponding secretary of the Down-and-Out Club.. I thought you could make a newspaper story out of it and win out a piece of money on general results. But, anyhow, don't you see that she's got to get back home before night?"

And then I began to feel that dull, leaden, soul-depressing sensation known as the sense of duty. Why should that sense fall upon one as a weight and a burden? I knew that I was doomed that day to give up the bulk of my store of hard-wrung coin to the relief of this Ada Lowery. But I swore to myself that Tripp's whiskey dollar would not be forthcoming. He might play knight-errant at my expense, but he would indulge in no wassail afterward, commemorating my weakness and gullibility. In a kind of chilly anger I put on my coat and hat.

Tripp, submissive, cringing, vainly endeavoring to please, conducted me via the street-cars to the human pawn-shop of Mother McGinnis. I paid the fares. It seemed that the collodion-scented Don Quixote and the smallest minted coin were strangers.

Tripp pulled the bell at the door of the mouldly red-brick boarding-house. At its faint tinkle he paled, and crouched as a rabbit makes ready to spring away at the sound of a hunting-dog. I guessed what a life he had led, terror-haunted by the coming footsteps of landladies.

"Give me one of the dollars - quick!" he said.

The door opened six inches. Mother McGinnis stood there with white Eyes, they were white, I say and a yellow face, holding together at her throat with one hand a dingy pink flannel dressing-sack. Tripp thrust the dollar through the space without a word, and it bought us entry.

"She's in the parlor," said the McGinnis, turning the back of her sack upon us.

In the dim parlor a girl sat at the cracked marble centre-table weeping comfortably and eating gum-drops. She was a flawless beauty. Crying had only made her brilliant eyes brighter. When she crunched a gum-drop you thought only of the poetry of motion and envied the senseless confection. Eve at the age of five minutes must have been a ringer for Miss Ada Lowery at nineteen or twenty. I was introduced, and a gum-drop suffered neglect while she conveyed to me a naive interest, such as a puppy dog (a prize winner) might bestow upon a crawling beetle or a frog.

Tripp took his stand by the table, with the fingers of one hand spread upon it, as an attorney or a master of ceremonies might have stood. But he looked the master of nothing. His faded coat was buttoned high, as if it sought to be charitable to deficiencies of tie and linen.

I thought of a Scotch terrier at the sight of his shifty eyes in the glade between his tangled hair and beard. For one ignoble moment I felt ashamed of having been introduced as his friend in the presence of so much beauty in distress. But evidently Tripp meant to conduct the ceremonies, whatever they might be. I thought I detected in his actions and pose an intention of foisting the situation upon me as material for a newspaper story, in a lingering hope of extracting from me his whiskey dollar.

"My friend" (I shuddered), "Mr. Chalmers," said Tripp, "will tell you, Miss Lowery, the same that I did. He's a reporter, and he can hand out the talk better than I can. That's why I brought him with me." (0 Tripp, wasn't it the silver-tongued orator you wanted?) "He's wise to a lot of things, and he'll tell you now what's best to do."

I stood on one foot, as it were, as I sat in my rickety chair.

"Why – er - Miss Lowery," I began, secretly enraged at Tripp's awkward opening, "I am at your service, of course, but - er - as I haven't been apprized of the circumstances of the case, I – er -"

"Oh," said Miss Lowery, beaming for a moment, "it ain't as bad as That, there ain't any circumstances. It's the first time I've ever been in New York except once when I was five years old, and I had no idea it was such a big town. And I met Mr. - Mr. Snip on the street and asked him about a friend of mine, and he brought me here and asked me to wait."

"I advise you, Miss Lowery," said Tripp, "to tell Mr. Chalmers all. He's a friend of mine" (I was getting used to it by this time), "and he'll give you the right tip."

"Why, certainly," said Miss Ada, chewing a gum-drop toward me. "There ain't anything to tell except that, well, everything's fixed for me to marry Hiram Dodd next Thursday evening. Hi has got two hundred acres of land with a lot of shore-front, and one of the best truck-farms on the Island. But this morning I had my horse saddled up - he's a white horse named Dancer - and I rode over to the station. I told 'em at home I was going to spend the day with Susie Adams. It was a story, I guess, but I don't care. And I came to New York on the train, and I met Mr. - Mr. Flip on the street and asked him if he knew where I could find G – G -"

"Now, Miss Lowery," broke in Tripp, loudly, and with much bad taste, I thought, as she hesitated with her word, "you like this young man, Hiram Dodd, don't you? He's all right, and good to you, ain't he?"

"Of course I like him," said Miss Lowery emphatically. "Hi's all right. And of course he's good to me. So is everybody."

I could have sworn it myself. Throughout Miss Ada Lowery's life all men would be to good to her. They would strive, contrive, struggle, and compete to hold umbrellas over her hat, check her trunk, pick up her handkerchief, buy for her soda at the fountain.

"But," went on Miss Lowery, "last night got to thinking about G - George, and I -"

Down went the bright gold head upon dimpled, clasped hands on the table. Such a beautiful April storm! Unrestrainedly sobbed. I wished I could have comforted her. But I was not George. And I was glad I was not Hiram and yet I was sorry, too.

By-and-by the shower passed. She straightened up, brave and half-way smiling. She would have made a splendid wife, for crying only made her eyes more bright and tender. She took a gum-drop and began her story.

"I guess I'm a terrible hayseed," she said between her little gulps and sighs, "but I can't help it. G - George Brown and I were sweethearts since he was eight and I was five. When he was nineteen - that was four years ago - he left Greenburg and went to the city. He said he was going to be a policeman or a railroad president or something. And then he was coming back for me. But I never heard from him any more. And I - I - liked him."

Another flow of tears seemed imminent, but Tripp hurled himself into the crevasse and dammed it. Confound him, I could see his game. He was trying to make a story of it for his sordid ends and profit.

"Go on, Mr. Chalmers," said he, "and tell the lady what's the proper caper. That's what I told her, you'd hand it to her straight. Spiel up."

I coughed, and tried to feel less wrathful toward Tripp. I saw my duty. Cunningly I had been inveigled, but I was securely trapped. Tripp's first dictum to me had been just and correct. The young lady must be sent back to Greenburg that day. She must be argued with, convinced, assured, instructed, ticketed, and returned without delay. I hated Hiram and despised George; but duty must be done.

Noblesse oblige and only five silver dollars are not strictly romantic compatibles, but sometimes they can be made to jibe. It was mine to be Sir Oracle, and then pay the freight. So I assumed an air that mingled Solomon's with that of the general passenger agent of the Long Island Railroad.

"Miss Lowery," said I, as impressively as I could, "life is rather a queer proposition, after all." There was a familiar sound to these words after I had spoken them, and I hoped Miss Lowery had never heard Mr. Cohan's song. "Those whom we first love we seldom wed. Our earlier romances, tinged with the magic radiance of youth, often fail to materialize." The last three words sounded somewhat trite when they struck the air. "But those fondly cherished dreams," I went on, "may cast a pleasant afterglow on our future lives, however impracticable and vague they may have been. But life is full of realities as well as visions and dreams. One cannot live on memories. May I ask, Miss Lowery, if you think you could pass a happy, that is, a contented and harmonious life with Mr. – er – Dodd - if in other ways than romantic recollections he seems to – er - fill the bill, as I might say?"

"Oh, Hi's all right," answered Miss Lowery. "Yes, I could get along with him fine. He's promised me an automobile and a motor-boat. But somehow, when it got so close to the time I was to marry him, I couldn't help wishing, well, just thinking about George. Something must have happened to him or he'd have written. On the day he left, he and me got a hammer and a chisel and cut a dime into two pieces. I took one piece and he took the other, and we promised to be true to each other and always keep the pieces till we saw each other again. I've got mine at home now in a ring-box in the top drawer of my dresser. I guess I was silly to come up here looking for him. I never realized what a big place it is."

And then Tripp joined in with a little grating laugh that he had, still trying to drag in a little story or drama to earn the miserable dollar that he craved.

"Oh, the boys from the country forget a lot when they come to the city and learn something. I guess George, maybe, is on the bum, or got roped in by some other girl, or maybe gone to the dogs on account of whiskey or the races. You listen to Mr. Chalmers and go back home, and you'll be all right."

But now the time was come for action, for the hands of the clock were moving close to noon. Frowning upon Tripp, I argued gently and philosophically with Miss Lowery, delicately convincing her of the importance of returning home at once. And I impressed upon her the truth that it would not be absolutely necessary to her future happiness that she mention to Hi the wonders or the fact of her visit to the city that had swallowed up the unlucky George.

She said she had left her horse (unfortunate Rosinante) tied to a tree near the railroad station. Tripp and I gave her instructions to mount the patient steed as soon as she arrived and ride home as fast as possible. There she was to recount the exciting adventure of a day spent with Susie Adams. She could "fix" Susie - I was sure of that - and all would be well.

And then, being susceptible to the barbed arrows of beauty, I warmed to the adventure. The three of us hurried to the ferry, and there I found the price of a ticket to Greenburg to be but a dollar and eighty cents. I bought one, and a red, red rose with the twenty cents for Miss Lowery. We saw her aboard her ferryboat, and stood watching her wave her handkerchief at us until it was the tiniest white patch imaginable. And then Tripp and I faced each other, brought back to earth, left dry and desolate in the shade of the sombre verities of life.

The spell wrought by beauty and romance was dwindling. I looked at Tripp and almost sneered. He looked more careworn, contemptible, and disreputable than ever. I fingered the two silver dollars remaining in my pocket and looked at him with the half-closed eyelids of contempt. He mustered up an imitation of resistance.

"Can't you get a story out of it?" he asked, huskily. "Some sort of a story, even if you have to fake part of it?"

"Not a line," said I. "I can fancy the look on Grimes' face if I should try to put over any slush like this. But we've helped the little lady out, and that'll have to be our only reward."

"I'm sorry," said Tripp, almost inaudibly. "I'm sorry you're out your money. Now, it seemed to me like a find of a big story, you know - that is, a sort of thing that would write up pretty well."

"Let's try to forget it," said I, with a praiseworthy attempt at gayety, "and take the next car 'cross town."

I steeled myself against his unexpressed but palpable desire. He should not coax, cajole, or wring from me the dollar he craved. I had had enough of that wild-goose chase.

Tripp feebly unbuttoned his coat of the faded pattern and glossy seams to reach for something that had once been a handkerchief deep down in some obscure and cavernous pocket. As he did so I caught the shine of a cheap silver-plated watch-chain across his vest, and something dangling from it caused me to stretch forth my hand and seize it curiously. It was the half of a silver dime that had been cut in halves with a chisel.

"What!" I said, looking at him keenly.

"Oh yes," he responded, dully. "George Brown, alias Tripp. what's the use?"

Barring the W. C. T. U., I'd like to know if anybody disapproves of my having produced promptly from my pocket Tripp's whiskey dollar and unhesitatingly laying it in his hand.

THE HIGHER PRAGMATISM

I

Where to go for wisdom has become a question of serious import. The ancients are discredited; Plato is boiler-plate; Aristotle is tottering; Marcus Aurelius is reeling; Aesop has been copyrighted by

Indiana; Solomon is too solemn; you couldn't get anything out of
Epictetus with a pick.

The ant, which for many years served as a model of intelligence and
industry in the school-readers, has been proven to be a doddering
idiot and a waster of time and effort. The owl to-day is hooted at.
Chautauqua conventions have abandoned culture and adopted diabolo.
Graybeards give glowing testimonials to the venders of patent hair-
restorers. There are typographical errors in the almanacs published
by the daily newspapers. College professors have become -

But there shall be no personalities. To sit in classes, to delve into
the encyclopedia or the past-performances page, will not make us wise.
As the poet says, "Knowledge comes, but wisdom lingers." Wisdom is
dew, which, while we know it not, soaks into us, refreshes us, and
makes us grow. Knowledge is a strong stream of water turned on us
through a hose. It disturbs our roots.

Then, let us rather gather wisdom. But how to do so requires
knowledge. If we know a thing, we know it; but very often we are not
wise to it that we are wise, and -

But let's go on with the story.

II

Once upon a time I found a ten-cent magazine lying on a bench in a
little city park. Anyhow, that was the amount he asked me for when I
sat on the bench next to him. He was a musty, dingy, and tattered
magazine, with some queer stories bound in him, I was sure. He turned
out to be a scrap-book.

"I am a newspaper reporter," I said to him, to try him. "I have been
detailed to write up some of the experiences of the unfortunate ones
who spend their evenings in this park. May I ask you to what you
attribute your downfall in -"

I was interrupted by a laugh from my purchase, a laugh so rusty and
unpractised that I was sure it had been his first for many a day.

"Oh, no, no," said he. "You ain't a reporter. Reporters don't talk
that way. They pretend to be one of us, and say they've just got in
on the blind baggage from St. Louis. I can tell a reporter on sight.
Us park bums get to be fine judges of human nature. We sit here all
day and watch the people go by. I can size up anybody who walks past
my bench in a way that would surprise you."

"Well," I said, "go on and tell me. How do you size me up?"

"I should say," said the student of human nature with unpardonable hesitation, "that you was, say, in the contracting business or maybe worked in a store - or was a sign-painter. You stopped in the park to finish your cigar, and thought you'd get a little free monologue out of me. Still, you might be a plasterer or a lawyer, it's getting kind of dark, you see. And your wife won't let you smoke at home."

I frowned gloomily.

"But, judging again," went on the reader of men, "I'd say you ain't got a wife."

"No," said I, rising restlessly. "No, no, no, I ain't. But I will have, by the arrows of Cupid! That is, if -"

My voice must have trailed away and muffled itself in uncertainty and despair.

"I see you have a story yourself," said the dusty vagrant impudently, it seemed to me. "Suppose you take your dime back and spin your yarn for me. I'm interested myself in the ups and downs of unfortunate ones who spend their evenings in the park."

Somehow, that amused me. I looked at the frowsy derelict with more interest. I did have a story. Why not tell it to him? I had told none of my friends. I had always been a reserved and bottled-up man. It was psychical timidity or sensitiveness-perhaps both. And I smiled to myself in wonder when I felt an impulse to confide in this stranger and vagabond.

"Jack," said I.

"Mack," said he.

"Mack," said I, "I'll tell you."

"Do you want the dime back in advance ?" said he.

I handed him a dollar.

"The dime," said I, "was the price of listening to your story."

"Right on the point of the jaw," said he. "Go on."

And then, incredible as it may seem to the lovers in the world who confide their sorrows only to the night wind and the gibbous moon, I laid bare my secret to that wreck of all things that you would have supposed to be in sympathy with love.

I told him of the days and weeks and months that I had spent in adoring Mildred Telfair. I spoke of my despair, my grievous days and wakeful nights, my dwindling hopes and distress of mind. I even pictured to this night-prowler her beauty and dignity, the great sway she had in society, and the magnificence of her life as the elder daughter of an ancient race whose pride overbalanced the dollars of the city's millionaires.

"Why don't you cop the lady out?" asked Mack, bringing me down to earth and dialect again.

I explained to him that my worth was so small, my income so minute, and my fears so large that I hadn't the courage to speak to her of my worship. I told him that in her presence I could only blush and stammer, and that she looked upon me with a wonderful, maddening smile of amusement.

"She kind of moves in the professional class, don't she?" asked Mack.

"The Telfair family -" I began, haughtily.

"I mean professional beauty," said my hearer.

"She is greatly and widely admired," I answered, cautiously.

"Any sisters?"

"One."

"You know any more girls?"

"Why, several," I answered. "And a few others."

"Say," said Mack, "tell me one thing, can you hand out the dope to other girls? Can you chin 'em and make matinee eyes at 'em and squeeze 'em? You know what I mean. You're just shy when it comes to this particular dame, the professional beauty, ain't that right ?"

"In a way you have outlined the situation with approximate truth," I admitted.

"I thought so," said Mack, grimly. "Now, that reminds me of my own case. I'll tell you about it."

I was indignant, but concealed it. What was this loafer's case or anybody's case compared with mine? Besides, I had given him a dollar and ten cents.

"Feel my muscle," said my companion, suddenly, flexing his biceps. I did so mechanically. The fellows in gyms are always asking you to do that. His arm was as hard as cast-iron.

"Four years ago," said Mack, "I could lick any man in New York outside of the professional ring. Your case and mine is just the same. I come from the West Side, between Thirtieth and Fourteenth, I won't give the number on the door. I was a scrapper when I was ten, and when I was twenty no amateur in the city could stand up four rounds with me. 'S a fact. You know Bill McCarty? No? He managed the smokers for some of them swell clubs. Well, I knocked out everything Bill brought up before me. I was a middle-weight, but could train down to a welter when necessary. I boxed all over the West Side at bouts and benefits and private entertainments, and was never put out once.

"But, say, the first time I put my foot in the ring with a professional I was no more than a canned lobster. I dunno how it was - I seemed to lose heart. I guess I got too much imagination. There was a formality and publieness about it that kind of weakened my nerve. I never won a fight in the ring. Light-weights and all kinds of scrubs used to sign up with my manager and then walk up and tap me on the wrist and see me fall. The minute I seen the crowd and a lot of gents in evening clothes down in front, and seen a professional come inside the ropes, I got as weak as ginger-ale.

"Of course, it wasn't long till I couldn't get no backers, and I didn't have any more chances to fight a professional or many amateurs, either. But lemme tell you, I was as good as most men inside the ring or out. It was just that dumb, dead feeling I had when I was up against a regular that always done me up.

"Well, sir, after I had got out of the business, I got a mighty grouch on. I used to go round town licking private citizens and all kinds of unprofessionals just to please myself. I'd lick cops in dark streets and car-conductors and cab-drivers and draymen whenever I could start a row with 'em. It didn't make any difference how big they were, or how much science they had, I got away with 'em. If I'd only just have had the confidence in the ring that I had beating up the best men outside of it, I'd be wearing black pearls and heliotrope silk socks to-day.

"One evening I was walking along near the Bowery, thinking about things, when along comes a slumming-party. About six or seven they was, all in swallowtails, and these silk hats that don't shine. One of the gang kind of shoves me off the sidewalk. I hadn't had a scrap in three days, and I just says, 'De-lighted!' and hits him back of the ear.

"Well, we had it. That Johnnie put up as decent a little fight as you'd want to see in the moving pictures. It was on a side street, and no cops around. The other guy had a lot of science, but it only took me about six minutes to lay him out.

"Some of the swallowtails dragged him up against some steps and began to fan him. Another one of 'em comes over to me and says:

"'Young man, do you know what you've done?'

"'Oh, beat it,' says I. 'I've done nothing but a little punching-bag work. Take Freddy back to Yale and tell him to quit studying sociology on the wrong side of the sidewalk.'

"'My good fellow,' says he, 'I don't know who you are, but I'd like to. You've knocked out Reddy Burns, the champion middle-weight of the world! He came to New York yesterday, to try to get a match on with Jim Jeifries. If you -'

"But when I come out of my faint I was laying on the floor in a drug-store saturated with aromatic spirits of ammonia. If I'd known that was Reddy Burns, I'd have got down in the gutter and crawled past him instead of handing him one like I did. Why, if I'd ever been in a ring and seen him climbing over the ropes, I'd have been all to the sal volatile.

"So that's what imagination does," concluded Mack. "And, as I said, your case and mine is simultaneous. You'll never win out. You can't go up against the professionals. I tell you, it's a park bench for yours in this romance business."

Mack, the pessimist, laughed harshly.

"I'm afraid I don't see the parallel," I said, coldly. "I have only a very slight acquaintance with the prize-ring."

The derelict touched my sleeve with his forefinger, for emphasis, as he explained his parable.

"Every man," said he, with some dignity, "has got his lamps on something that looks good to him. With you, it's this dame that you're afraid to say your say to. With me, it was to win out in the ring. Well, you'll lose just like I did."

"Why do you think I shall lose?" I asked warmly.

"'Cause," said he, "you're afraid to go in the ring. You dassen't stand up before a professional. Your case and mine is just the same. You're a amateur; and that means that you'd better keep outside of the ropes."

"Well, I must be going," I said, rising and looking with elaborate care at my watch.

When I was twenty feet away the park-bencher called to me.

"Much obliged for the dollar," he said. "And for the dime. But you'll never get 'er. You're in the amateur class."

"Serves you right," I said to myself, "for hobnobbing with a tramp. His impudence!"

But, as I walked, his words seemed to repeat themselves over and over again in my brain. I think I even grew angry at the man.

"I'll show him!" I finally said, aloud. "I'll show him that I can fight Reddy Burns, too - even knowing who he is."

I hurried to a telephone-booth and rang up the Telfair residence.

A soft, sweet voice answered. Didn't I know that voice? My hand holding the receiver shook.

"Is that you?" said I, employing the foolish words that form the vocabulary of every talker through the telephone.

"Yes, this is I," came back the answer in the low, clear-cut tones that are an inheritance of the Telfairs. "Who is it, please?"

"It's me," said I, less ungrammatically than egotistically. "It's me, and I've got a few things that I want to say to you right now and immediately and straight to the point."

"Dear me," said the voice. "Oh, it's you, Mr. Arden!"

I wondered if any accent on the first word was intended; Mildred was fine at saying things that you had to study out afterward.

"Yes," said I. "I hope so. And now to come down to brass tacks." I thought that rather a vernacularism, if there is such a word, as soon as I had said it; but I didn't stop to apologize. "You know, of course, that I love you, and that I have been in that idiotic state for a long time. I don't want any more foolishness about it - that is, I mean I want an answer from you right now. Will you marry me or not? Hold the wire, please. Keep out, Central. Hello, hello! Will you, or will you not.?"

That was just the uppercut for Reddy Burns' chin. The answer came back:

"Why, Phil, dear, of course I will! I didn't know that you - that is, you never said - oh, come up to the house, please - I can't say what I want to over the 'phone. You are so importunate. But please come up to the house, won't you?"

Would I?

I rang the bell of the Telfair house violently. Some sort of a human came to the door and shooed me into the drawing-room.

"Oh, well," said I to myself, looking at the ceiling, "anyone can learn from any one. That was a pretty good philosophy of Mack's, anyhow. He didn't take advantage of his experience, but I get the benefit of it. If you want to get into the professional class, you've got to -"

I stopped thinking then. Someone was coming down the stairs. My knees began to shake. I knew then how Mack had felt when a professional began to climb over the ropes.

I looked around foolishly for a door or a window by which I might escape. If it had been any other girl approaching, I mightn't have. But just then the door opened, and Bess, Mildred's younger sister, came in. I'd never seen her look so much like a glorified angel. She walked straight tip to me, and - and - I'd never noticed before what perfectly wonderful eyes and hair Elizabeth Telfair had.

"Phil," she said, in the Telfair, sweet, thrilling tones, "why didn't you tell me about it before? I thought it was sister you wanted all the time, until you telephoned to me a few minutes ago!"

I suppose Mack and I always will be hopeless amateurs. But, as the thing has turned out in my case, I'm mighty glad of it.

BEST-SELLER

I

One day last summer I went to Pittsburgh, well, I had to go there on business.

My chair-car was profitably well filled with people of the kind one usually sees on chair-cars. Most of them were ladies in brown-silk dresses cut with square yokes, with lace insertion, and dotted veils, who refused to have the windows raised. Then there was the usual number of men who looked as if they might be in almost any business and going almost anywhere. Some students of human nature can look at a man in a Pullman and tell you where he is from, his occupation and his stations in life, both flag and social; but I never could. The only way I can correctly judge a fellow-traveller is when the train is held up by robbers, or when he reaches at the same time I do for the last towel in the dressing-room of the sleeper.

The porter came and brushed the collection of soot on the window-sill off to the left knee of my trousers. I removed it with an air of apology. The temperature was eighty-eight. One of the dotted-veiled ladies demanded the closing of two more ventilators, and spoke loudly of Interlaken. I leaned back idly in chair No. 7, and looked with the tepidest curiosity at the small, black, bald-spotted head just visible above the back of No. 9.

Suddenly No. 9 hurled a book to the floor between his chair and the window, and, looking, I saw that it was The Rose-Lady and Trevelyan, one of the best-selling novels of the present day. And then the critic or Philistine, whichever he was, veered his chair toward the window, and I knew him at once for John A. Pescud, of Pittsburgh, travelling salesman for a plate-glass company, an old acquaintance whom I had not seen in two years.

In two minutes we were faced, had shaken hands, and had finished with such topics as rain, prosperity, health, residence, and destination. Politics might have followed next; but I was not so ill-fated.

I wish you might know John A. Pescud. He is of the stuff that heroes are not often lucky enough to be made of. He is a small man with a wide smile, and an eye that seems to be fixed upon that little red spot on the end of your nose. I never saw him wear but one kind of necktie, and he believes in cuff-holders and button-shoes. He is as hard and true as anything ever turned out by the Cambria Steel Works; and he believes that as soon as Pittsburgh makes smoke-consumers compulsory, St. Peter will come down and sit at the foot of Smithfield Street, and let somebody else attend to the gate up in the branch heaven. He believes that "our" plate-glass is the most important commodity in the world, and that when a man is in his home town he ought to be decent and law-abiding.

During my acquaintance with him in the City of Diurnal Night I had never known his views on life, romance, literature, and ethics. We had browsed, during our meetings, on local topics, and then parted, after Chateau Margaux, Irish stew, flannel-cakes, cottage-pudding, and coffee (hey, there! with milk separate). Now I was to get more of his ideas. By way of facts, he told me that business had picked up since the party conventions, and that he was going to get off at Coketown.

II

"Say," said Pescud, stirring his discarded book with the toe of his right shoe, "did you ever read one of these best-sellers? I mean the kind where the hero is an American swell - sometimes even from Chicago - who falls in love with a royal princess from Europe who is travelling under an alias, and follows her to her father's kingdom or principality? I guess you have. They're all alike. Sometimes this going-away masher is a Washington newspaper correspondent, and sometimes he is a Van Something from New York, or a Chicago wheat-broker worthy fifty millions. But he's always ready to break into the king row of any foreign country that sends over their queens and princesses to try the new plush seats on the Big Four or the B. and 0. There doesn't seem to be any other reason in the book for their being here.

"Well, this fellow chases the royal chair-warmer home, as I said, and finds out who she is. He meets here on the corso or the strasse one evening and gives us ten pages of conversation. She reminds him of the difference in their stations, and that gives him a chance to ring in three solid pages about America's uncrowned sovereigns. If you'd take his remarks and set 'em to music, and then take the music away from 'em, they'd sound exactly like one of George Cohan's songs.

"Well, you know how it runs on, if you ve read any of 'em, he slaps the king's Swiss body-guards around like everything whenever they get in his way. He's a great fencer, too. Now, I've known of some Chicago men who were pretty notorious fences, but I never heard of any fencers coming from there. He stands on the first landing of the royal staircase in Castle Schutzenfestenstein with a gleaming rapier in his hand, and makes a Baltimore broil of six platoons of traitors who come to massacre the said king. And then he has to fight duels with a couple of chancellors, and foil a plot by four Austrian archdukes to seize the kingdom for a gasoline-station.

"But the great scene is when his rival for the princess' hand, Count Feodor, attacks him between the portcullis and the ruined chapel, armed with a mitrailleuse, a yataghan, and a couple of Siberian bloodhounds. This scene is what runs the best-seller into the twenty-ninth edition before the publisher has had time to draw a check for the advance royalties.

"The American hero shucks his coat and throws it over the heads of the bloodhounds, gives the mitrailleuse a slap with his mitt, says 'Yah!' to the yataghan, and lands in Kid McCoy's best style on the count's left eye. Of course, we have a neat little prize-fight right then and there. The count, in order to make the go possible, seems to be an expert at the art of self-defence, himself; and here we have the Corbett-Sullivan fight done over into literature. The book ends with the broker and the princess doing a John Cecil Clay cover under the linden-trees on the Gorgonzola Walk. That winds up the love-story plenty good enough. But I notice that the book dodges the final issue. Even a best-seller has sense enough to shy at either leaving a Chicago grain broker on the throne of Lobsterpotsdam or bringing over a real princess to eat fish and potato salad in an Italian chalet on Michigan Avenue. What do you think about 'em?"

"Why," said I, "I hardly know, John. There's a saying: 'Love levels all ranks,' you know."

"Yes," said Pescud, "but these kind of love-stories are rank, on the level. I know something about literature, even if I am in plate-glass. These kind of books are wrong, and yet I never go into a train but what they pile 'em up on me. No good can come out of an international clinch between the Old-World aristocracy and one of us fresh Americans. When people in real life marry, they generally hunt up somebody in their own station. A fellow usually picks out a girl that went to the same high-school and belonged to the same singing-society that he did. When young millionaires fall in love, they always select the chorus-girl that likes the same kind of sauce on the lobster that he does. Washington newspaper correspondents always many widow ladies ten years older than themselves who keep boarding-houses.

No, sir, you can't make a novel sound right to me when it makes one of C. D. Gibson's bright young men go abroad and turn kingdoms upside down just because he's a Taft American aud took a course at a gymnasium. And listen how they talk, too!"

Pescud picked up the best-seller and hunted his page.

"Listen at this," said he. "Trevelyan is chinning with the Princess Alwyna at the back end of the tulip-garden. This is how it goes:

"'Say not so, dearest and sweetest of earth's fairest flowers. Would I aspire? You are a star set high above me in a royal heaven; I am Only myself. Yet I am a man, and I have a heart to do and dare. I have no title save that of an uncrowned sovereign; but I have an arm and a sword that yet might free Schutzenfestenstein from the plots of traitors.'

"Think of a Chicago man packing a sword, and talking about freeing anything that sounded as much like canned pork as that! He'd be much more likely to fight to have an import duty put on it."

"I think I understand you, John," said I. "You want fiction-writers to be consistent with their scenes and characters. They shouldn't mix Turkish pashas with Vermont farmers, or English dukes with Long Island clam-diggers, or Italian countesses with Montana cowboys, or Cincinnati brewery agents with the rajahs of India."

"Or plain business men with aristocracy high above 'em," added Pescud. "It don't jibe. People are divided into classes, whether we admit it or not, and it's everybody's impulse to stick to their own class. They do it, too. I don't see why people go to work and buy hundreds of thousands of books like that. You don't see or hear of any such didoes and capers in real life."

III

"Well, John," said I, "I haven't read a best-seller in a long time. Maybe I've had notions about them somewhat like yours. But tell me more about yourself. Getting along all right with the company?"

"Bully," said Pescud, brightening at once. "I've had my salary raised twice since I saw you, and I get a commission, too. I've bought a neat slice of real estate out in the East End, and have run up a house on it. Next year the firm is going to sell me some shares of stock. Oh, I'm in on the line of General Prosperity, no matter who's elected!"

"Met your affinity yet, John?" I asked.

"Oh, I didn't tell you about that, did I?" said Pescud with a broader grin.

"0-ho!" I said. "So you've taken time enough off from your plate-glass to have a romance?"

"No, no," said John. "No romance, nothing like that! But I'll tell you about it.

"I was on the south-bound, going to Cincinnati, about eighteen months ago, when I saw, across the aisle, the finest-looking girl I'd ever laid eyes on. Nothing spectacular, you know, but just the sort you want for keeps. Well, I never was up to the flirtation business, either handkerchief, automobile, postage-stamp, or door-step, and she wasn't the kind to start anything. She read a book and minded her business, which was to make the world prettier and better just by residing on it. I kept on looking out of the side doors of my eyes, and finally the proposition got out of the Pullman class into a case of a cottage with a lawn and vines running over the porch. I never thought of speaking to her, but I let the plate-glass business go to smash for a while.

"She changed cars at Cincinnati, and took a sleeper to Louisville over the L. and N. There she bought another ticket, and went on through Shelbyville, Frankfort, and Lexington. Along there I began to have a hard time keeping up with her. The trains came along when they pleased, and didn't seem to be going anywhere in particular, except to keep on the track and the right of way as much as possible. Then they began to stop at junctions instead of towns, and at last they stopped altogether. I'll bet Pinkerton would outbid the plate-glass people for my services any time if they knew how I managed to shadow that young lady. I contrived to keep out of her sight as much as I could, but I never lost track of her.

"The last station she got off at was away down in Virginia, about six in the afternoon. There were about fifty houses and four hundred niggers in sight. The rest was red mud, mules, and speckled hounds.

"A tall old man, with a smooth face and white hair, looking as proud as Julius Caesar and Roscoe Conkling on the same post-card, was there to meet her. His clothcs were frazzled, but I didn't notice that till later. He took her little satchel, and they started over the plank-walks and went up a road along the hill. I kept along a piece behind 'em, trying to look like I was hunting a garnet ring in the sand that my sister had lost at a picnic the previous Saturday.

"They went in a gate on top of the hill. It nearly took my breath away when I looked up. Up there in the biggest grove I ever saw was a tremendous house with round white pillars about a thousand feet high, and the yard was so full of rose-bushes and box-bushes and lilacs that you couldn't have seen the house if it hadn't been as big as the Capitol at Washington.

"'Here's where I have to trail,' says I to myself. "I thought before that she seemed to be in moderate circumstances, at least. This must be the Governor's mansion, or the Agricultural Building of a new

World's Fair, anyhow. I'd better go back to the village and get posted by the postmaster, or drug the druggist for some information.

"In the village I found a pine hotel called the Bay View House. The only excuse for the name was a bay horse grazing in the front yard. I set my sample-case down, and tried to be ostensible. I told the landlord I was taking orders for plate-glass.

"'I don't want no plates,' says he, 'but I do need another glass molasses-pitcher.'

"By-and-by I got him down to local gossip and answering questions.

"'Why,' says he, 'I thought everybody knowed who lived in the big white house on the hill. It's Colonel Allyn, the biggest man and the finest quality in Virginia, or anywhere else. They're the oldest family in the State. That was his daughter that got off the train. She's been up to Illinois to see her aunt, who is sick.'

"I registered at the hotel, and on the third day I caught the young lady walking in the front yard, down next to the paling fence. I stopped and raised my hat, there wasn't any other way.

"'Excuse me,' says I, 'can you tell me where Mr. Hinkle lives?'

"She looks at me as cool as if I was the man come to see about the weeding of the garden, but I thought I saw just a slight twinkle of fun in her eyes.

"'No one of that name lives in Birchton,' says she. 'That is,' she goes on, 'as far as I know. Is the gentleman you are seeking white?'

"Well, that tickled me. 'No kidding,' says I. 'I'm not looking for smoke, even if I do come from Pittsburgh.'

"'You are quite a distance from home,' says she.

"'I'd have gone a thousand miles farther,' says I.

"'Not if you hadn't waked up when the train started in Shelbyville,' says she; and then she turned almost as red as one of the roses on the bushes in the yard. I remembered I had dropped off to sleep on a bench in the Shelbyville station, waiting to see which train she took, and only just managed to wake up in time.

"And then I told her why I had come, as respectful and earnest as I could. And I told her everything about myself, and what I was making, and how that all I asked was just to get acquainted with her and try to get her to like me.

"She smiles a little, and blushes some, but her eyes never get mixed up. They look straight at whatever she's talking to.

"'I never had any one talk like this to me before, Mr. Pescud,' says she. 'What did you say your name is, John?'

"'John A.,' says I.

"'And you came mighty near missing the train at Powhatan Junction, too,' says she, with a laugh that sounded as good as a mileage-book to me.

"'How did you know?' I asked.

"'Men are very clumsy,' said she. 'I knew you were on every train. I thought you were going to speak to me, and I'm glad you didn't.'

"Then we had more talk; and at last a kind of proud, serious look came on her face, and she turned and pointed a finger at the big house.

"'The Allyns,' says she, 'have lived in Elmcroft for a hundred years. We are a proud family. Look at that mansion. It has fifty rooms. See the pillars and porches and balconies. The ceilings in the reception-rooms and the ball-room are twenty-eight feet high. My father is a lineal descendant of belted earls.'

"'I belted one of 'em once in the Duquesne Hotel, in Pittsburgh,' says I, 'and he didn't offer to resent it. He was there dividing his attentions between Monongahela whiskey and heiresses, and he got fresh.'

"'Of course,' she goes on, 'my father wouldn't allow a drummer to set his foot in Elmeroft. If he knew that I was talking to one over the fence he would lock me in my room.'

"'Would you let me come there?' says I. 'Would you talk to me if I was to call? For,' I goes on, 'if you said I might come and see you, the earls might be belted or suspendered, or pinned up with safety-pins, as far as I am concerned.'

"'I must not talk to you,' she says, 'because we have not been introduced. It is not exactly proper. So I will say good-bye, Mr. -'
"'Say the name,' says I. 'You haven't forgotten it.'

"'Pescud,' says she, a little mad.

"'The rest of the name!' I demands, cool as could be.

"'John,' says she.

"'John - what?' I says.

"'John A.,' says she, with her head high. 'Are you through, now?'

"'I'm coming to see the belted earl to-morrow,' I says.

"'He'll feed you to his fox-hounds,' says she, laughing.

"'If he does, it'll improve their running,' says I. 'I'm something of a hunter myself.'

"'I must be going in now,' says she. 'I oughtn't to have spoken to you at all. I hope you'll have a pleasant trip back to Minneapolis or Pittsburgh, was it? Good-bye!'

"'Good-night,' says I, 'and it wasn't Minneapolis. What's your name, first, please?'

"She hesitated. Then she pulled a leaf off a bush, and said:

"'My name is Jessie,' says she.

"'Good-night, Miss Allyn,' says I.

"The next morning at eleven, sharp, I rang the door-bell of that World's Fair main building. After about three-quarters of an hour an old nigger man about eighty showed up and asked what I wanted. I gave him my business card, and said I wanted to see the colonel. He showed me in.

"Say, did you ever crack open a wormy English walnut? That's what that house was like. There wasn't enough furniture in it to fill an eight-dollar flat. Some old horsehair lounges and three-legged chairs and some framed ancestors on the walls were all that met the eye. But when Colonel Allyn comes in, the place seemed to light up. You could almost hear a band playing, and see a bunch of old-timers in wigs and white stockings dancing a quadrille. It was the style of him, although he had on the same shabby clothes I saw him wear at the station.

"For about nine seconds he had me rattled, and I came mighty near getting cold feet and trying to sell him some plate-glass. But I got my nerve back pretty quick. He asked me to sit down, and I told him everything. I told him how I followed his daughter from Cincinnati, and what I did it for, and all about my salary and prospects, and explained to him my little code of living to be always decent and right in your home town; and when you're on the road, never take more than four glasses of beer a day or play higher than a twenty-five-cent limit. At first I thought he was going to throw me out of the window, but I kept on talking. Pretty soon I got a chance to tell him that story about the Western Congressman who had lost his pocket-book and the grass widow, you remember that story. Well, that got him to laughing, and I'll bet that was the first laugh those ancestors and horsehair sofas had heard in many a day.

"We talked two hours. I told him everything I knew; and then he began to ask questions, and I told him the rest. All I asked of him was to give me a chance. If I couldn't make a hit with the little lady, I'd clear out, and not bother any more. At last he says:

"'There was a Sir Courtenay Pescud in the time of Charles I, if I remember rightly.'

"'If there was,' says I, 'he can't claim kin with our bunch. We've always lived in and around Pittsburgh. I've got an uncle in the real-estate business, and one in trouble somewhere out in Kansas. You can inquire about any of the rest of us from anybody in old Smoky Town, and get satisfactory replies. Did you ever run across that story about the captain of the whaler who tried to make a sailor say his prayers?' says I.

"'It occurs to me that I have never been so fortunate,' says the colonel.

"So I told it to him. Laugh! I was wishing to myself that he was a customer. What a bill of glass I'd sell him! And then he says:

"'The relating of anecdotes and humorous occurrences has always seemed to me, Mr. Pescud, to be a particularly agreeable way of promoting and perpetuating amenities between friends. With your permission, I will relate to you a fox-hunting story with which I was personally connected, and which may furnish you some amusement.'

So he tells it. It takes forty minutes by the watch. Did I laugh? Well, say! When I got my face straight he calls in old Pete, the super-annuated darky, and sends him down to the hotel to bring up my valise. It was Elmcroft for me while I was in the town.

"Two evenings later I got a chance to speak a word with Miss Jessie alone on the porch while the colonel was thinking up another story.

"'It's going to be a fine evening,' says I.

"'He's coming,' says she. 'He's going to tell you, this time, the story about the old negro and the green watermelons. It always comes after the one about the Yankees and the game rooster. There was another time,' she goes on, 'that you nearly got left, it was at Pulaski City.'

"'Yes,' says I, 'I remember. My foot slipped as I was jumping on the step, and I nearly tumbled off.'

"'I know,' says she. 'And - and I - I was afraid you had, John A. I was afraid you had.'

"And then she skips into the house through one of the big windows."

IV

"Coketown!" droned the porter, making his way through the slowing car.

Pescud gathered his hat and baggage with the leisurely promptness of an old traveller.

"I married her a year ago," said John. "I told you I built a house in the East End. The belted, I mean the colonel, is there, too. I find him waiting at the gate whenever I get back from a trip to hear any new story I might have picked up on the road."

I glanced out of the window. Coketown was nothing more than a ragged hillside dotted with a score of black dismal huts propped up against dreary mounds of slag and clinkers. It rained in slanting torrents, too, and the rills foamed and splashed down through the black mud to the railroad-tracks.

"You won't sell much plate-glass here, John," said I. "Why do you get off at this end-o'-the-world?"

"Why," said Pescud, "the other day I took Jessie for a little trip to Philadelphia, and coming back she thought she saw some petunias in a pot in one of those windows over there just like some she used to raise down in the old Virginia home. So I thought I'd drop off here for the night, and see if I could dig up some of the cuttings or blossoms for her. Here we are. Good-night, old man. I gave you the address. Come out and see us when you have time."

The train moved forward. One of the dotted brown ladies insisted on having windows raised, now that the rain beat against them. The porter came along with his mysterious wand and began to light the car.

I glanced downward and saw the best-seller. I picked it up and set it carefully farther along on the floor of the car, where the rain-drops would not fall upon it. And then, suddenly, I smiled, and seemed to see that life has no geographical metes and bounds.

"Good-luck to you, Trevelyan," I said. "And may you get the petunias for your princess!"

RUS IN URBE

Considering men in relation to money, there are three kinds whom I dislike: men who have more money than they can spend; men who have more money than they do spend; and men who spend more money than they have. Of the three varieties, I believe I have the least liking for the first. But, as a man, I liked Spencer Grenville North pretty well, although he had something like two or ten or thirty millions - I've forgotten exactly how many.

I did not leave town that summer. I usually went down to a village on the south shore of Long Island. The place was surrounded by duck-farms, and the ducks and dogs and whippoorwills and rusty windmills made so much noise that I could sleep as peacefully as if I were in my own flat six doors from the elevated railroad in New York. But that summer I did not go. Remember that. One of my friends asked me why I did not. I replied:

"Because, old man, New York is the finest summer resort in the world." You have heard that phrase before. But that is what I told him.

I was press-agent that year for Binkly & Bing, the theatrical managers and producers. Of course you know what a press-agent is. Well, he is not. That is the secret of being one.

Binkly was touring France in his new C. & N. Williamson car, and Bing had gone to Scotland to learn curling, which he seemed to associate in his mind with hot tongs rather than with ice. Before they left they gave me June and July, on salary, for my vacation, which act was in accord with their large spirit of liberality. But I remained in New York, which I had decided was the finest summer resort in -

But I said that before.

On July the 10th, North came to town from his camp in the Adirondacks. Try to imagine a camp with sixteen rooms, plumbing, eiderdown quilts, a butler, a garage, solid silver plate, and a long-distance telephone. Of course it was in the woods, if Mr. Pinchot wants to preserve the forests let him give every citizen two or ten or thirty million dollars, and the trees will all gather around the summer camps, as the Birnam woods came to Dunsinane, and be preserved.

North came to see me in my three rooms and bath, extra charge for light when used extravagantly or all night. He slapped me on the back (I would rather have my shins kicked any day), and greeted me with out-door obstreperousness and revolting good spirits. He was insolently brown and healthy-looking, and offensively well dressed.

"Just ran down for a few days," said he, "to sign some papers and stuff like that. My lawyer wired me to come. Well, you indolent cockney, what are you doing in town? I took a chance and telephoned, and they said you were here. What's the matter with that Utopia on Long Island where you used to take your typewriter and your villanous temper every summer? Anything wrong with the – er - swans, weren't they, that used to sing on the farms at night?"

"Ducks," said I. "The songs of swans are for luckier ears. They swim and curve their necks in artificial lakes on the estates of the wealthy to delight the eyes of the favorites of Fortune."

"Also in Central Park," said North, "to delight the eyes of immigrants and bummers. I've seen em there lots of times. But why are you in the city so late in the summer?"

"New York City," I began to recite, "is the finest sum -"

"No, you don't," said North, emphatically. "You don't spring that old one on me. I know you know better. Man, you ought to have gone up with us this summer. The Prestons are there, and Tom Volney and the Monroes and Lulu Stanford and the Miss Kennedy and her aunt that you liked so well."

"I never liked Miss Kennedy's aunt," I said.

"I didn't say you did," said North. "We are having the greatest time we've ever had. The pickerel and trout are so ravenous that I believe they would swallow your hook with a Montana copper-mine prospectus fastened on it. And we've a couple of electric launches; and I'll tell you what we do every night or two - we tow a rowboat behind each one with a big phonograph and a boy to change the discs in 'em. On the water, and twenty yards behind you, they are not so bad. And there are passably good roads through the woods where we go motoring. I shipped two cars up there. And the Pinecliff Inn is only three miles away. You know the Pinecliff. Some good people are there this season, and we run over to the dances twice a week. Can't you go back with me for a week, old man?"

I laughed. "Northy," said I "if I may be so familiar with a millionaire, because I hate both the names Spencer and Grenville - your invitation is meant kindly, but the city in the summer-time for me. Here, while the bourgeoisie is away, I can live as Nero lived-barring, thank heaven, the fiddling-while the city burns at ninety in the shade. The tropics and the zones wait upon me like handmaidens. I sit under Florida palms and eat pomegranates while Boreas himself, electrically conjured up, blows upon me his Arctic breath. As for trout, you know, yourself, that Jean, at Maurice's, cooks them better than anyone else in the world."

"Be advised," said North. "My chef has pinched the blue ribbon from the lot. He lays some slices of bacon inside the trout, wraps it all in corn-husks, the husks of green corn, you know, buries them in hot ashes and covers them with live coals. We build fires on the bank of the lake and have fish suppers."

"I know," said I. "And the servants bring down tables and chairs and damask cloths, and you eat with silver forks. I know the kind of camps that you millionaires have. And there are champagne pails set about, disgracing the wild flowers, and, no doubt, Madame Tetrazzini to sing in the boat pavilion after the trout."

"Oh no," said North, concernedly, "we were never as bad as that. We did have a variety troupe up from the city three or four nights, but they weren't stars by as far as light can travel in the same length of time. I always like a few home comforts even when I'm roughing it. But don't tell me you prefer to stay in the city during summer. I don't believe it. If you do, why did you spend your summers there for the last four years, even sneaking away from town on a night train, and refusing to tell your friends where this Arcadian village was?"

"Because," said I, "they might have followed me and discovered it. But since then I have learned that Amaryllis has come to town. The coolest things, the freshest, the brightest, the choicest, are to be found in the city. If you've nothing on hand this evening I will show you."

"I'm free," said North, "and I have my light car outside. I suppose, since you've been converted to the town, that your idea of rural sport is to have a little whirl between bicycle cops in Central Park and then a mug of sticky ale in some stuffy rathskeller under a fan that can't stir up as many revolutions in a week as Nicaragua can in a day."

"We'll begin with the spin through the Park, anyhow," I said. I was choking with the hot, stale air of my little apartment, and I wanted that breath of the cool to brace me for the task of proving to my friend that New York was the greatest and so forth.

"Where can you find air any fresher or purer than this?" I asked, as we sped into Central's boskiest dell.

"Air!" said North, contemptuously. "Do you call this air? this muggy vapor, smelling of garbage and gasoline smoke. Man, I wish you could get one sniff of the real Adirondack article in the pine woods at daylight."

"I have heard of it," said I. "But for fragrance and tang and a joy in the nostrils I would not give one puff of sea breeze across the bay, down on my little boat dock on Long Island, for ten of your turpentine-scented tornadoes."

"Then why," asked North, a little curiously, "don't you go there instead of staying cooped up in this Greater Bakery?"

"Because," said I, doggedly, "I have discovered that New York is the greatest summer -"

"Don't say that again," interrupted North, "unless you've actually got a job as General Passenger Agent of the Subway. You can't really believe it."

I went to some trouble to try to prove my theory to my friend. The Weather Bureau and the season had conspired to make the argument worthy of an able advocate.

The city seemed stretched on a broiler directly above the furnaces of Avernus. There was a kind of tepid gayety afoot and awheel in the boulevards, mainly evinced by languid men strolling about in straw hats and evening clothes, and rows of idle taxicabs with their flags up, looking like a blockaded Fourth of July procession. The hotels kept up a specious brilliancy and hospitable outlook, but inside one saw vast empty caverns, and the footrails at the bars gleamed brightly from long disacquaintance with the sole-leather of customers. In the cross-town streets the steps of the old brownstone houses were swarming with "stoopers," that motley race hailing from sky-light room and basement, bringing out their straw doorstep mats to sit and fill the air with strange noises and opinions.

North and I dined on the top of a hotel; and here, for a few minutes, I thought I had made a score. An east wind, almost cool, blew across the roofless roof. A capable orchestra concealed in a bower of wistaria played with sufficient judgment to make the art of music probable and the art of conversation possible.

Some ladies in reproachless summer gowns at other tables gave animation and color to the scene. And an excellent dinner, mainly from the refrigerator, seemed to successfully back my judgment as to summer resorts. But North grumbled all during the meal, and cursed his lawyers and prated so of his confounded camp in the woods that I began to wish he would go back there and leave me in my peaceful city retreat.

After dining we went to a roof-garden vaudeville that was being much praised. There we found a good bill, an artificially cooled atmosphere, cold drinks, prompt service, and a gay, well-dressed audience. North was bored.

"If this isn't comfortable enough for you on the hottest August night for five years," I said, a little sarcastically, "you might think about the kids down in Delancey and Hester streets lying out on the fire-escapes with their tongues hanging out, trying to get a breath of air that hasn't been fried on both sides. The contrast might increase your enjoyment."

"Don't talk Socialism," said North. "I gave five hundred dollars to the free ice fund on the first of May. I'm contrasting these stale, artificial, hollow, wearisome 'amusements' with the enjoyment a man can get in the woods. You should see the firs and pines do skirt-dances during a storm; and lie down flat and drink out of a mountain branch at the end of a day's tramp after the deer. That's the only way to spend a summer. Get out and live with nature."

"I agree with you absolutely," said I, with emphasis.

For one moment I had relaxed my vigilance, and had spoken my true sentiments. North looked at me long and curiously.

"Then why, in the name of Pan and Apollo," he asked, "have you been singing this deceitful paean to summer in town?"

I suppose I looked my guilt.

"Ha," said North, "I see. May I ask her name?"

"Annie Ashton," said I, simply. "She played Nannette in Binkley &
Bing's production of The Silver Cord. She is to have a better part
next season."

"Take me to see her," said North.

Miss Ashton lived with her mother in a small hotel. They were out of
the West, and had a little money that bridged the seasons. As press-
agent of Binkley & Bing I had tried to keep her before the public. As
Robert James Vandiver I had hoped to withdraw her; for if ever one was
made to keep company with said Vandiver and smell the salt breeze on
the south shore of Long Island and listen to the ducks quack in the
watches of the night, it was the Ashton set forth above.

But she had a soul above ducks, above nightingales; aye, even above
birds of paradise. She was very beautiful, with quiet ways, and
seemed genuine. She had both taste and talent for the stage, and she
liked to stay at home and read and make caps for her mother. She was
unvaryingly kind and friendly with Binkley & Bing's press-agent.
Since the theatre had closed she had allowed Mr. Vandiver to call in
an unofficial role. I had often spoken to her of my friend, Spencer
Grenville North; and so, as it was early, the first turn of the
vaudeville being not yet over, we left to find a telephone.

Miss Ashton would be very glad to see Mr. Vandiver and Mr. North.

We found her fitting a new cap on her mother. I never saw her look
more charming.

North made himself disagreeably entertaining. He was a good talker,
and had a way with him. Besides, he had two, ten, or thirty millions,
I've forgotten which. I incautiously admired the mother's cap,
whereupon she brought out her store of a dozen or two, and I took a
course in edgings and frills. Even though Annie's fingers had pinked,
or ruched, or hemmed, or whatever you do to 'em, they palled upon me.
And I could hear North drivelling to Annie about his odious Adirondack
camp.

Two days after that I saw North in his motor-car with Miss Ashton and
her mother. On the next afternoon he dropped in on me.

"Bobby," said he, "this old burg isn't such a bad proposition in the
summer-time, after all. Since I've keen knocking around it looks
better to me. There are some first-rate musical comedies and light
operas on the roofs and in the outdoor gardens. And if you hunt up
the right places and stick to soft drinks, you can keep about as cool

here as you can in the country. Hang it! when you come to think of it, there's nothing much to the country, anyhow. You get tired and sunburned and lonesome, and you have to eat any old thing that the cook dishes up to you."

"It makes a difference, doesn't it?" said I.

"It certainly does. Now, I found some whitebait yesterday, at Maurice's, with a new sauce that beats anything in the trout line I ever tasted."

"It makes a difference, doesn't it?" I said.

"Immense. The sauce is the main thing with whitebait."

"It makes a difference, doesn't it?" I asked, looking him straight in the eye. He understood.

"Look here, Bob," he said, "I was going to tell you. I couldn't help it. I'll play fair with you, but I'm going in to win. She is the 'one particular' for me."

"All right," said I. "It's a fair field. There are no rights for you to encroach upon."

On Thursday afternoon Miss Ashton invited North and myself to have tea in her apartment. He was devoted, and she was more charming than usual. By avoiding the subject of caps I managed to get a word or two into and out of the talk. Miss Ashton asked me in a make conversational tone something about the next season's tour.

"Oh," said I, "I don't know about that. I'm not going to be with Binkley & Bing next season."

"Why, I thought," said she, "that they were going to put the Number One road company under your charge. I thought you told me so."

"They were," said I, "but they won't.. I'll tell you what I'm going to do. I'm going to the south shore of Long Island and buy a small cottage I know there on the edge of the bay. And I'll buy a catboat and a rowboat and a shotgun and a yellow dog. I've got money enough to do it. And I'll smell the salt wind all day when it blows from the sea and the pine odor when it blows from the land. And, of course, I'll write plays until I have a trunk full of 'em on hand.

"And the next thing and the biggest thing I'll do will be to buy that duck-farm next door. Few people understand ducks. I can watch 'em for hours. They can march better than any company in the National Guard, and they can play 'follow my leader' better than the entire Democratic party. Their voices don't amount to much, but I like to hear 'em. They wake you up a dozen times a night, but there's a homely sound about their quacking that is more musical to me than the cry of 'Fresh strawber-rees!' under your window in the morning when you want to sleep.

"And," I went on, enthusiastically, "do you know the value of ducks besides their beauty and intelligence and order and sweetness of voice? Picking their feathers gives you an unfailing and never ceasing income. On a farm that I know the feathers were sold for $400 in one year. Think of that! And the ones shipped to the market will bring in more money than that. Yes, I am for the ducks and the salt breeze coming over the bay. I think I shall get a Chinaman cook, and with him and the dog and the sunsets for company I shall do well. No more of this dull, baking, senseless, roaring city for me."

Miss Ashton looked surprised. North laughed.

"I am going to begin one of my plays tonight," I said, "so I must be going." And with that I took my departure.

A few days later Miss Ashton telephoned to me, asking me to call at four in the afternoon.

I did.

"You have been very good to me," she said, hesitatingly, "and I thought I would tell you. I am going to leave the stage."

"Yes," said I, "I suppose you will. They usually do when there's so much money."

"There is no money," she said, "or very little. Our money is almost gone."

"But I am told," said I, "that he has something like two or ten or thirty millions - I have forgotten which."

"I know what you mean," she said. "I will not pretend that I do not. I am not going to marry Mr. North."

"Then why are you leaving the stage ?" I asked, severely. "What else can you do to earn a living?"

She came closer to me, and I can see the look in her eyes yet as she spoke.

"I can pick ducks," she said.

We sold the first year's feathers for $350.

A POOR RULE

I have always maintained, and asserted ime to time, that woman is no mystery; that man can foretell, construe, subdue, comprehend, and interpret her. That she is a mystery has been foisted by herself upon credulous mankind. Whether I am right or wrong we shall see. As "Harper's Drawer" used to say in bygone years: "The following good story is told of Miss -, Mr. -, Mr. - and Mr. -."

We shall have to omit "Bishop X" and "the Rev. -," for they do not belong.

In those days Paloma was a new town on the line of the Southern Pacific. A reporter would have called it a "mushroom" town; but it was not. Paloma was, first and last, of the toadstool variety.

The train stopped there at noon for the engine to drink and for the passengers both to drink and to dine. There was a new yellow-pine hotel, also a wool warehouse, and perhaps three dozen box residences. The rest was composed of tents, cow ponies, "black-waxy" mud, and mesquite-trees, all bound round by a horizon. Paloma was an about-to-be city. The houses represented faith; the tents hope; the twice-a-day train by which you might leave, creditably sustained the role of charity.

The Parisian Restaurant occupied the muddlest spot in the town while it rained, and the warmest when it shone. It was operated, owned, and perpetrated by a citizen known as Old Man Hinkle, who had come out of Indiana to make his fortune in this land of condensed milk and sorghum.

There was a four-room, unpainted, weather-boarded box house in which the family lived. From the kitchen extended a "shelter" made of poles covered with chaparral brush. Under this was a table and two benches, each twenty feet long, the product of Paloma home carpentry. Here was set forth the roast mutton, the stewed apples, boiled beans, soda-biscuits, puddinorpie, and hot coffee of the Parisian menu.

Ma Hinkle and a subordinate known to the ears as "Betty," but denied to the eyesight, presided at the range. Pa Hinkle himself, with salamandrous thumbs, served the scalding viands. During rush hours a

Mexican youth, who rolled and smoked cigarettes between courses, aided him in waiting on the guests. As is customary at Parisian banquets, I place the sweets at the end of my wordy menu.

Ileen Hinkle!

The spelling is correct, for I have seen her write it. No doubt she had been named by ear; but she so splendidly bore the orthography that Tom Moore himself (had he seen her) would have indorsed the phonography.

Ileen was the daughter of the house, and the first Lady Cashier to invade the territory south of an east-and-west line drawn through Galveston and Del Rio. She sat on a high stool in a rough pine grand-Stand or was it a temple? under the shelter at the door of the kitchen. There was a barbed-wire protection in front of her, with a little arch under which you passed your money. Heaven knows why the barbed wire; for every man who dined Parisianly there would have died in her service. Her duties were light; each meal was a dollar; you put it under the arch, and she took it.

I set out with the intent to describe Ileen Hinkle to you. Instead, I must refer you to the volume by Edmund Burke entitled: A Philosophical Inquiry into the Origin of Our Ideas of the Sublime and Beautiful. It is an exhaustive treatise, dealing first with the primitive conceptions of beauty, roundness and smoothness, I think they are, according to Burke. It is well said. Rotundity is a patent charm; as for smoothness the more new wrinkles a woman acquires, the smoother she becomes.

Ileen was a strictly vegetable compound, guaranteed under the Pure Ambrosia and Balm-of-Gilead Act of the year of the fall of Adam. She was a fruit-stand blonde-strawberries, peaches, cherries, etc. Her eyes were wide apart, and she possessed the calm that precedes a storm that never comes. But it seems to me that words (at any rate per) are wasted in an effort to describe the beautiful. Like fancy, "It is engendered in the eyes." There are three kinds of beauties, I was foreordained to be homiletic; I can never stick to a story.

The first is the freckle-faced, snub-nosed girl whom you like. The second is Maud Adams. The third is, or are, the ladies in Bouguereau's paintings. Ileen Hinkle was the fourth. She was the mayoress of Spotless Town. There were a thousand golden apples coming to her as Helen of the Troy laundries.

The Parisian Restaurant was within a radius. Even from beyond its circumference men rode in to Paloma to win her smiles. They got them. One meal - one smile - one dollar. But, with all her impartiality,

Ileen seemed to favor three of her admirers above the rest. According to the rules of politeness, I will mention myself last.

The first was an artificial product known as Bryan Jacks, a name that had obviously met with reverses. Jacks was the outcome of paved cities. He was a small man made of some material resembling flexible sandstone. His hair was the color of a brick Quaker meeting-house; his eyes were twin cranberries; his mouth was like the aperture under a drop-letters-here sign.

He knew every city from Bangor to San Francisco, thence north to Portland, thence S. 45 E. to a given point in Florida. He had mastered every art, trade, game, business, profession, and sport in the world, had been present at, or hurrying on his way to, every head-line event that had ever occurred between oceans since he was five years old. You might open the atlas, place your finger at random upon the name of a town, and Jacks would tell you the front names of three prominent citizens before you could close it again. He spoke patronizingly and even disrespectfully of Broadway, Beacon Hill, Michigan, Euclid, and Fifth avenues, and the St. Louis Four Courts. Compared with him as a cosmopolite, the Wandering Jew would have seemed a mere hermit. He had learned everything the world could teach him, and he would tell you about it.

I hate to be reminded of Pollock's Course of Time, and so do you; but every time I saw Jacks I would think of the poet's description of another poet by the name of G. G. Byron who "Drank early; deeply drank, drank draughts that common millions might have quenched; then died of thirst because there was no more to drink."

That fitted Jacks, except that, instead of dying, he came to Paloma, which was about the same thing. He was a telegrapher and station-and express-agent at seventy-five dollars a month. Why a young man who knew everything and could do everything was content to serve in such an obscure capacity I never could understand, although he let out a hint once that it was as a personal favor to the president and stockholders of the S. P. Ry. Co.

One more line of description, and I turn Jacks over to you. He wore bright blue clothes, yellow shoes, and a bow tie made of the same cloth as his shirt.

My rival No.2 was Bud Cunningham, whose services had been engaged by a ranch near Paloma to assist in compelling refractory cattle to keep within the bounds of decorum and order. Bud was the only cowboy off the stage that I ever saw who looked like one on it. He wore the sombrero, the chaps, and the handkerchief tied at the back of his neck.

Twice a week Bud rode in from the Val Verde Ranch to sup at the Parisian Restaurant. He rode a many-high-handed Kentucky horse at a tremendously fast lope, which animal he would rein up so suddenly under the big mesquite at the corner of the brush shelter that his hoofs would plough canals yards long in the loam.

Jacks and I were regular boarders at the restaurant, of course.

The front room of the Hinkle House was as neat a little parlor as there was in the black-waxy country. It was all willow rocking-chairs, and home-knit tidies, and albums, and conch shells in a row. And a little upright piano in one comer.

Here Jacks and Bud and I, or sometimes one or two of us, according to our good-luck, used to sit of evenings when the tide of trade was over, and "visit" Miss Hinkle.

Ileen was a girl of ideas. She was destined for higher things (if there can be anything higher) than taking in dollars all day through a barbed-wire wicket. She had read and listened and thought. Her looks would have formed a career for a less ambitious girl; but, rising superior to mere beauty, she must establish something in the nature of a salon, the only one in Paloma.

"Don't you think that Shakespeare was a great writer?" she would ask, with such a pretty little knit of her arched brows that the late Ignatius Donnelly, himself, had he seen it, could scarcely have saved his Bacon.

Ileen was of the opinion, also, that Boston is more cultured than Chicago; that Rosa Bonheur was one of the greatest of women painters; that Westerners are more spontaneous and open-hearted than Easterners; that London must be a very foggy city, and that California must be quite lovely in the springtime. And of many other opinions indicating a keeping up with the world's best thought.

These, however, were but gleaned from hearsay and evidence: Ileen had theories of her own. One, in particular, she disseminated to us untiringly. Flattery she detested. Frankness and honesty of speech and action, she declared, were the chief mental ornaments of man and woman. If ever she could like any one, it would be for those qualities.

"I'm awfully weary," she said, one evening, when we three musketeers of the mesquite were in the little parlor, "of having compliments on my looks paid to me. I know I'm not beautiful."

(Bud Cunningham told me afterward that it was all he could do to keep from calling her a liar when she said that.)

"I'm only a little Middle-Western girl," went on Ileen, "who justs wants to be simple and neat, and tries to help her father make a humble living."

(Old Man Hinkle was shipping a thousand silver dollars a month, clear profit, to a bank in San Antonio.)

Bud twisted around in his chair and bent the rim of his hat, from which he could never be persuaded to separate. He did not know whether she wanted what she said she wanted or what she knew she deserved. Many a wiser man has hesitated at deciding. Bud decided.

"Why, ah, Miss Ileen, beauty, as you might say, ain't everything. Not sayin' that you haven't your share of good looks, I always admired more than anything else about you the nice, kind way you treat your ma and pa. Any one what's good to their parents and is a kind of home-body don't specially need to be too pretty."

Ileen gave him one of her sweetest smiles. "Thank you, Mr. Cunningham," she said. "I consider that one of the finest compliments I've had in a long time. I'd so much rather hear you say that than to hear you talk about my eyes and hair. I'm glad you believe me when I say I don't like flattery."

Our cue was there for us. Bud had made a good guess. You couldn't lose Jacks. He chimed in next.

"Sure thing, Miss Ileen," he said; "the good-lookers don't always win out. Now, you ain't bad looking, of course-but that's nix-cum rous. I knew a girl once in Dubuque with a face like a cocoanut, who could skin the cat twice on a horizontal bar without changing hands. Now, a girl might have the California peach crop mashed to a marmalade and not be able to do that. I've seen – er - worse lookers than you, Miss Ileen; but what I like about you is the business way you've got of doing things. Cool and wise - that's the winning way for a girl. Mr. Hinkle told me the other day you'd never taken in a lead silver dollar or a plugged one since you've been on the job. Now, that's the stuff for a girl - that's what catches me."

Jacks got his smile, too.

"Thank you, Mr. Jacks," said Ileen. "If you only knew how I appreciate any one's being candid and not a flatterer! I get so tired of people telling me I'm pretty. I think it is the loveliest thing to have friends who tell you the truth."

Then I thought I saw an expectant look on Ileen's face as she glanced toward me. I had a wild, sudden impulse to dare fate, and tell her of all the beautiful handiwork of the Great Artificer she was the most exquisite - that she was a flawless pearl gleaming pure and serene in a setting of black mud and emerald prairies - that she was – a - a corker; and as for mine, I cared not if she were as crtiel as a serpent's tooth to her fond parents, or if she couldn't tell a plugged dollar from a bridle buckle, if I might sing, chant, praise, glorify, and worship her peerless and wonderful beauty.

But I refrained. I feared the fate of a flatterer. I had witnessed her delight at the crafty and discreet words of Bud and Jacks. No! Miss Hinkle was not one to be beguiled by the plated-silver tongue of a flatterer. So I joined the ranks of the candid and honest. At once I became mendacious and didactic.

"In all ages, Miss Hinkle," said I, "in spite of the poetry and romance of each, intellect in woman has been admired more than beauty. Even in Cleopatra, herself, men found more charm in her queenly mind than in her looks."

"Well, I should think so!" said Ileen. "I've seen pictures of her that weren't so much. she had an awfully long nose."

"If I may say so," I went on, "you remind me of Cleopatra, Miss Ileen."

"Why, my nose isn't so long!" said she, opening her eyes wide and touching that comely feature with a dimpled forefinger.

"Why – er - I mean," said I -" I mean as to mental endowments."

"Oh!" said she; and then I got my smile just as Bud and Jacks had got theirs.

"Thank every one of you," she said, very, very sweetly, "for being so frank and honest with me. That's the way I want you to be always. Just tell me plainly and truthfully what you think, and we'll all be the best friends in the world. And now, because you've been so good to me, and understand so well how I dislike people who do nothing but pay me exaggerated compliments, I'll sing and play a little for you."

Of course, we expressed our thanks and joy; but we would have been better pleased if Ileen had remained in her low rocking-chair face to face with us and let us gaze upon her. For she was no Adelina Patti -

not even on the fare-wellest of the diva's farewell tours. She had a
cooing little voice like that of a turtle-dove that could almost fill
the parlor when the windows and doors were closed, and Betty was not
rattling the lids of the stove in the kitchen. She had a gamut that I
estimate at about eight inches on the piano; and her runs and trills
sounded like the clothes bubbling in your grandmother's iron wash-pot.
Believe that she must have been beautiful when I tell you that it
sounded like music to us.

"She Must Have Been Beautiful When I Tell You That It Sounded Like
Music To Us"

Ileen's musical taste was catholic. She would sing through a pile of
sheet music on the left-hand top of the piano, laying each slaughtered
composition on the right-hand top. The next evening she would sing
from right to left. Her favorites were Mendelssohn, and Moody and
Sankey. By request she always wound up with Sweet Violets and When
the Leaves Begin to Turn.

When we left at ten o'clock the three of us would go down to Jacks'
little wooden station and sit on the platform, swinging our feet and
trying to pump one another for dews as to which way Miss Ileen's
inclinations seemed to lean. That is the way of rivals, they do not
avoid and glower at one another; they convene and converse and
construe, striving by the art politic to estimate the strength of the
enemy.

One day there came a dark horse to Paloma, a young lawyer who at once
flaunted his shingle and himself spectacularly upon the town. His
name was C. Vincent Vesey. You could see at a glance that he was a
recent graduate of a southwestern law school. His Prince Albert coat,
light striped trousers, broad-brimmed soft black hat, and narrow white
muslin bow tie proclaimed that more loudly than any diploma could.
Vesey was a compound of Daniel Webster, Lord Chesterfield, Beau
Brummell, and Little Jack Horner. His coming boomed Paloma. The next
day after he arrived an addition to the town was surveyed and laid off
in lots.

Of course, Vesey, to further his professional fortunes, must mingle
with the citizenry and outliers of Paloma. And, as well as with the
soldier men, he was bound to seek popularity with the gay dogs of the
place. So Jacks and Bud Cunningham and I came to be honored by his
acquaintance.

The doctrine of predestination would have been discredited had not
Vesey seen Ileen Hinkle and become fourth in the tourney.
Magnificently, he boarded at the yellow pine hotel instead of at the

Parisian Restaurant; but he came to be a formidable visitor in the Hinkle parlor. His competition reduced Bud to an inspired increase of profanity, drove Jacks to an outburst of slang so weird that it sounded more horrible than the most trenchant of Bud's imprecations, and made me dumb with gloom.

For Vesey had the rhetoric. Words flowed from him like oil from a gusher. Hyperbole, compliment, praise, appreciation, honeyed gallantry, golden opinions, eulogy, and unveiled panegyric vied with one another for pre-eminence in his speech. We had small hopes that Ileen could resist his oratory and Prince Albert.

But a day came that gave us courage.

About dusk one evening I was sitting on the little gallery in front of the Hinkle parlor, waiting for Ileen to come, when I heard voices inside. She had come into the room with her father, and Old Man Hinkle began to talk to her. I had observed before that he was a shrewd man, and not unphilosophic.

"Ily," said he, "I notice there's three or four young fellers that have been callin' to see you regular for quite a while. Is there any one of 'em you like better than another?"

"Why, pa," she answered, "I like all of 'em very well. I think Mr. Cuninngham and Mr. Jacks and Mr. Harris are very nice young men. They are so frank and honest in everything they say to me. I haven't known Mr. Vesey very long, but I think he's a very nice young man, he's so frank and honest in everything he says to me."

"Now, that's what I'm gittin' at," says old Hinkle. "You've always been sayin' you like people what tell the truth and don't go humbuggin' you with compliments and bogus talk. Now, suppose you make a test of these fellers, and see which one of 'em will talk the straightest to you."

"But how'll I do it, pa?"

"I'll tell you how. You know you sing a little bit, Ily; you took music-lessons nearly two years in Logansport. It wasn't long, but it was all we could afford then. And your teacher said you didn't have any voice, and it was a waste of money to keep on. Now, suppose you ask the fellers what they think of your singin', and see what each one of 'em tells you. The man that 'll tell you the truth about it 'll have a mighty lot of nerve, and 'll do to tie to. What do you think of the plan?"

"All right, pa," said Ileen. "I think it's a good idea. I'll try it."

Ileen and Mr. Hinkle went out of the room through the inside doors. Unobserved, I hurried down to the station. Jacks was at his telegraph table waiting for eight o'clock to come. It was Bud's night in town, and when he rode in I repeated the conversation to them both. I was loyal to my rivals, as all true admirers of all Ileens should be.

Simultaneously the three of us were smitten by an uplifting thought. Surely this test would eliminate Vesey from the contest. He, with his unctuous flattery, would be driven from the lists. Well we remembered Ileen's love of frankness and honesty, how she treasured truth and candor above vain compliment and blandishment.

Linking arms, we did a grotesque dance of joy up and down the platform, singing Muldoon Was a Solid Man at the top of our voices.

That evening four of the willow rocking-chairs were filled besides the lucky one that sustained the trim figure of Miss Hinkle. Three of us awaited with suppressed excitement the application of the test. It was tried on Bud first.

"Mr. Cunningham," said Ileen, with her dazzling smile, after she had sung When the Leaves Begin to Turn, "what do you really think of my voice? Frankly and honestly, now, as you know I want you to always be toward me."

Bud squirmed in his chair at his chance to show the sincerity that he knew was required of him.

"Tell you the truth, Miss Ileen," he said, earnestly, "you ain't got much more voice than a weasel, just a little squeak, you know. Of course, we all like to hear you sing, for it's kind of sweet and soothin' after all, and you look most as mighty well sittin' on the piano-stool as you do faced around. But as for real singin' I reckon you couldn't call it that."

I looked closely at Ileen to see if Bud had overdone his frankness, but her pleased smile and sweetly spoken thanks assured me that we were on the right track.

"And what do you think, Mr. Jacks?" she asked next.

"Take it from me," said Jacks, "you ain't in the prima donna class. I've heard 'em warble in every city in the United States; and I tell you your vocal output don't go. Otherwise, you've got the grand opera bunch sent to the soap factory in looks, I mean; for the high screechers generally look like Mary Ann on her Thursday out. But nix for the gargle work. Your epiglottis ain't a real side-stepper, its footwork ain't good."

With a merry laugh at Jacks' criticism, Ileen looked inquiringly at me.

I admit that I faltered a little. Was there not such a thing as being too frank? Perhaps I even hedged a little in my verdict; but I stayed with the critics.

"I am not skilled in scientific music, Miss Ileen," I said, "but, frankly, I cannot praise very highly the singing-voice that Nature has given you. It has long been a favorite comparison that a great singer sings like a bird. Well, there are birds and birds. I would say that your voice reminds me of the thrush's - throaty and not strong, nor of much compass or variety - but still – er – sweet – in - er - its - way, and - er -"

"Thank you, Mr. Harris," interrupted Miss Hinkle. "I knew I could depend Upon your frankness and honesty."

And then C. Vincent Vesey drew back one sleeve from his snowy cuff, and the water came down at Lodore.

My memory cannot do justice to his masterly tribute to that priceless, God-given treasure - Miss Hinkle's voice. He raved over it in terms that, if they had been addressed to the morning stars when they sang together, would have made that stellar choir explode in a meteoric shower of flaming self-satisfaction.

He marshalled on his white finger-tips the grand opera stars of all the continents, from Jenny Lind to Emma Abbott, only to depreciate their endowments. He spoke of larynxes, of chest notes, of phrasing, arpeggios, and other strange paraphernalia of the throaty art. He admitted, as though driven to a corner, that Jenny Lind had a note or two in the high register that Miss Hinkle had not yet acquired - but"!!!" - that was a mere matter of practice and training.

And, as a peroration, he predicted - solemnly predicted - a career in vocal art for the "coming star of the Southwest - and one of which grand old Texas may well be proud," hitherto unsurpassed in the annals of musical history.

When we left at ten, Ileen gave each of us her usual warm, cordial handshake, entrancing smile, and invitation to call again. I could not see that one was favored above or below another but three of us knew, we knew.

We knew that frankness and honesty had won, and that the rivals now numbered three instead of four.

Down at the station Jacks brought out a pint bottle of the proper stuff, and we celebrated the downfall of a blatant interloper.

Four days went by without anything happening worthy of recount.

On the fifth, Jacks and I, entering the brush arbor for our supper, saw the Mexican youth, instead of a divinity in a spotless waist and a navy-blue skirt, taking in the dollars through the barbed-wire wicket.

We rushed into the kitchen, meeting Pa Hinkle coming out with two cups of hot coffee in his hands.

"Where's Ileen?" we asked, in recitative.

Pa Hinkle was a kindly man. "Well, gents," said he, "it was a sudden notion she took; but I've got the money, and I let her have her way. She's gone to a corn - a conservatory in Boston for four years for to have her voice cultivated. Now, excuse me to pass, gents, for this coffee's hot, and my thumbs is tender."

That night there were four instead of three of us sitting on the station platform and swinging our feet. C. Vincent Vesey was one of us. We discussed things while dogs barked at the moon that rose, as big as a five-cent piece or a flour barrel, over the chaparral.

And what we discussed was whether it is better to lie to a woman or to tell her the truth.

And as all of us were young then, we did not come to a decision.

THE END